AMERICA'S G█
TASK F█
CODENA█

Drexell, William The man in command. Tough. Exacting. And with a love of action still great enough to propel him into the heart of the most dangerous Triad maneuver. Now he heads the most covert operations of the U.S. in every part of the globe—and in many ways, holds its future in his hand.

Lisker, James As tense as a cobra and as deadly. A martial arts expert, was all too well known for his guerrilla capabilities during the Vietnam War. The group's master of communications, he is equally at home decoding a piece of Russian intelligence and ''coaxing'' information out of reluctant enemy agents.

Hahn, Jerry His two year's in Navy intelligence barely prepared him for the grueling physical demands of Triad. A leading political analyst, he now can—and must—fight and survive the bloodiest guerrilla operations in the world.

Zoccola, John Lithe, dangerous, and good-looking. A street fighter from New York as proficient on the battlefield as he is in the world of international finance. Able to play any part and assume any role, he can be found in the thick of any Triad maneuver—often with a beautiful woman at his side.

THEIR MISSION: To fight America's enemies with brains, brawn and strategy. To use whatever means are necessary to protect the freedom of endangered nations and the security of the U.S. Call them spies, commandos, or masterminds—when the world's hot spots turn explosive, Triad is there.

COUNTDOWN WW III: OPERATION NORTH AFRICA

A Novel by W. X. Davies with the
Strategic Operations Group

BERKLEY BOOKS, NEW YORK

This is a work of fiction. The characters, incidents, places and dialogues are products of the author's imagination and are not to be construed as real. The author's use of names of actual persons, living or dead, is incidental to the purposes of the plot and is not intended to change the entirely fictional character of the work.

COUNTDOWN WW III:
OPERATION NORTH AFRICA

A Berkley Book / published by arrangement with
the author

PRINTING HISTORY
Berkley edition / March 1984

ISBN: 0–425–06563–4

PRINTED IN THE UNITED STATES OF AMERICA

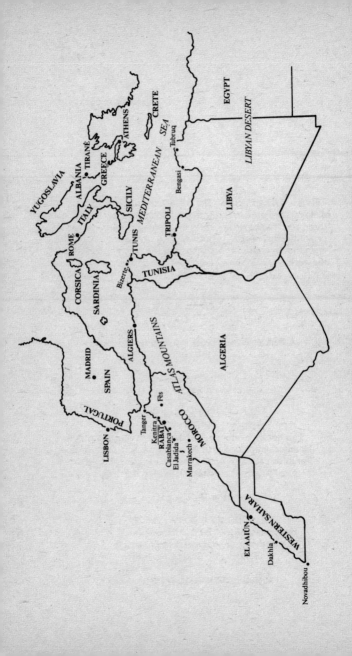

PROLOGUE

By early June of 1986 the power struggle between the United States and the Soviet Union has reached a point of combustion. Strategic arms talks in Geneva have been broken off and both superpowers are deploying a bewildering array of new weapons systems—cruise missiles, nuclear submarines, stealth bombers, high-energy laser satellites—in an increasingly desperate attempt to gain military advantage. While the NATO alliance is beset by political discord and debate over what to do about nuclear arms and structural unemployment—despite the temporary recovery of the mid-1980's—the Warsaw Pact nations are exhibiting signs of growing unrest that might one day develop into outright revolution.

For its part, the Soviet Union is experiencing severe economic strain, having reaped the harvest of years of failed five-year plans, inclement weather in the agricultural heartland, declining prices for gold and oil on the world market, and a rigid centralized bureaucracy.

In an attempt to counter the buildup of arms by the

West and to preserve their influence in the Third World, the Russians have taken more and more to supporting surrogate forces against American-backed armies. Even as warfare continues in Cambodia, Afghanistan, El Salvador, and Angola, the Soviet leaders seek new arenas in the world where they can challenge their capitalist rivals.

But who exactly is running the Soviet Union? By late spring of 1986 it has become impossible for U.S. intelligence experts to determine which man is in charge. A power struggle has enveloped the Kremlin for weeks, and whether the technocrats who sit on the Politburo will emerge victorious or yield in favor of the Red Army or the KGB is anyone's guess.

A year and a half in office, U.S. President Creighton Turner has favored a steady but uninspired foreign policy. Preoccupied by domestic problems, he had hoped to escape the kind of crises and upheavals in international affairs that had dogged his predecessors. But he is soon to discover that his cautious approach is misplaced, that if he doesn't act quickly and decisively, he will lose much more than just the next election . . .

METRIC TOP SECRET OP OP OP
PRESIDENTIAL DIRECTIVE 1414
From: President
To: Secretary of State/Secretary of Defense/
        National Security Advisor
02118B February 14, 1986

      TOTALITY.   All ack. personally.

1.   In light of the aggravated tensions around the
      world, instigated and inflamed by the Soviet

Union and its client states, the need for a new intelligence unit, answerable directly to the President of the United States, has become an urgent necessity.

2. This unit shall function as a small, close-knit group composed of individuals expert in political, economic, communications, and intelligence affairs.

3. Its purpose shall be to pinpoint those regions of the world where an international crisis is most likely to arise; to formulate contingency plans to prevent the crisis from occurring; and to arrest the crisis if it does occur.

4. In the event that direct intervention, requiring clandestine action on the part of the unit, is deemed necessary, the President shall have the power to mandate such intervention.

5. The name of this intelligence unit shall be the Global Crisis Task Force. In view of the three-pronged nature of the Global Crisis Task Force's mission, its code name shall be Triad.

Signed *Creighton Turner*,
        President of the United States

1

There was dead silence in the Launch Control Center of the National Security Agency. Sixteen men, uniformly dressed in white shirts and dark slacks, sat at a bank of consoles distinguished by a television monitor. It was two-thirty on the morning of July 18, but here in the control center, for all practical purposes, there was no time. Shifts changed, personnel came and went, but no one was really aware of the time outside in the Maryland countryside; the only time that mattered was satellite time, surveillance time.

Three nights before, an American satellite code-named Secsat DV-2—known more commonly to Mission Control simply as "The Bird"—had been launched in the nose of a Titan IIIC rocket. At T plus 2562 seconds the Titan had delivered the Bird to transfer orbit, an elliptical path that took it two thousand two hundred miles above the surface of the earth.

In the course of the last seventy-two hours the Secsat had made several shakedown passes around the globe,

4

allowing ground stations in Zamengoe, Cameroon; Carnarvon, Australia; Tangua, Brazil; and Ponta Delgada in the Azores to track it.

It was now on its tenth pass; at the farthest point along this pass Mission Control intended to initiate a crucial maneuver, apogee motor firing (AMF), which would propel the Bird forty miles out and into a round, geosynchronous orbit that would keep it fixed above the northern tier of Africa.

Seated in a chair that held a view of the bank of consoles was the present Director of Mission Control, Spencer Ross. A portly man with the look of a pugilist some years out of the ring, Ross could only guess at the purpose of Secsat DV-2. It wasn't his business to know, of course, only to keep the Bird in the orbit it was programmed for, but he had served long enough with the National Security Agency to venture an opinion about Secsat. Given the specifications for its orbit, which would permanently place it above Libya and Tunisia, he deduced that its most likely objective was to maintain surveillance of any military movements in the area. He also judged that the satellite would be equipped with formidable communications hardware, permitting it to relay back previously unobtainable information.

Now, however, Ross's attention was exclusively on the apogee motor firing. It would last only forty-two seconds, but in that short span of time any number of things could go wrong, the most dreaded of which were that the Bird would wander off into an unwanted orbit or backfire and blow itself up.

In spite of the dangers of the maneuver, the mood at Mission Control was one of routine procedures accomplished in a relaxed atmosphere. Every half-second three Hewlett-Packard minicomputers smoothly processed several hundred bits of information being relayed into Launch Control from Secsat DV-2. The technicians assembled by the data consoles exchanged routine-sounding messages through their lightweight headphones, and every now and then someone would cease his chatter to sip from a can of Coke or take a bite from a sandwich ordered up from the commissary downstairs. On the wall over the monitors, a succession of digital clocks ticked off Greenwich Mean Time as well as the times at the various tracking stations around the world. The only clock enjoying much attention, however, was the one showing how many seconds remained until AMF.

The change in orbit was scheduled for T plus 77:05 hours, which was five minutes away. Ross, leaning back in his reclining chair, ordered a check of all systems.

Within thirty seconds one of the technicians reported back to him that all systems were go. In a moment confirmation of this was radioed to the ground station in El Jadida, on the Atlantic coast of Morocco.

"We read you clearly, Ross," came the reply through the Director's earphones. It was delivered in barely accented English.

Ross failed to recognize the voice. "Is that you, Housni?" he asked sharply, referring to Housni Shobokshi, head of the ground control station at El Jadida, with whom Ross was accustomed to dealing.

"No, this is Ibrahim Brega. Mr. Shobokshi is in poor health this morning. I am in charge today."

"All right then," Ross replied after overcoming his initial surprise. "Please turn on the enabling switch."

Several monitors were now tuned to Channel 6, the channel for El Jadida, and the image on these monitors was duplicated on a large screen that dominated much of the center wall. In addition, the orbital image was now being shared by monitors at both Mission Control and El Jadida. When the signal to fire was passed to the satellite from the Moroccan tracking station, both places would know instantly if the firing was a success.

It was now two minutes before firing, and Ross began his final check on the status of the Bird, checking out eight channels in all. When he saw that everything continued to go as scheduled, he forced himself to sit back.

The last minute before firing seemed to stretch on forever, and Ross's face tensed in anticipation as he strained to catch whatever message might come through the static-charged channel from El Jadida.

After the final minute had passed without any message, Ross's patience disappeared entirely.

"Mr. Brega? Mr. Brega!" Ross growled into his mouthpiece.

Silence except for static.

Then, "This is Ibrahim Brega. Our solutions seem to agree." Ross looked up at the large screen. It showed the new, corrected orbit in place.

Before he could relax, however, a new radio message from Morocco broke the silence.

"Ross? This is Ibrahim Brega again."

"What is it?" Ross said sharply. He had just glanced up at the large screen; the line representing the satellite's orbit had zigzagged off the edge of the graph. His first hope was that something had gone wrong, not with the satellite, but with the computer monitoring it.

"I regret that we have lost contact with Secsat DV-2," said the apologetic voice.

"What? What are you saying?" Ross shouted, although there was no need to, since the audio technology would allow a whisper to be heard in Morocco.

Brega repeated his unhappy message.

"Well," Ross demanded, "then where the hell has it gone? Was there any trouble with the firing?"

At the same time Ross was asking this question, the technicians at Mission Control were already attempting to discover the answer by punching queries into their computer consoles.

"As far as I can determine, sir, the apogee motor firing proceeded perfectly. You could see that for yourself," he added, sounding affronted that Ross could even suggest that there might have been a problem. And it was true; the AMF had gone off without a hitch. But then, where was the satellite? It had accurately moved into the higher, geosynchronous orbit, but then it had just disappeared. Satellites, Ross knew, could go crazy or blow themselves up, but they didn't just disappear.

"What the hell is going on there, Brega?" Ross demanded in angry frustration.

There was no response.

"Mr. Brega, I asked you a question. *What is going on over there?*"

He was answered by a high-pitched whining sound as the line went dead.

2

Jerry Hahn was completely lost, and the laser beams slicing through the predawn darkness were of little help, revealing only intermittently a half-ton GAZ field car and a pair of MT-LB armored personnel carriers on the rise of an unidentifiable, tree-covered hill behind him. Artillery fire rumbled in the distance.

As bullets traced through the air, whistling past his shoulder, he began to weave as he ran away from the approaching vehicles. Without thinking, he suddenly threw himself on the ground, which was soggy from the night-long downpour that was only now letting up.

Sprawled on the swampy ground, Hahn could barely discern the barbed wire just up ahead, shrouded as it was by the laser-lit smoke. He dug a map out of his camouflage jacket pocket and tried to read it by the feeble illumination from his flashlight.

But he couldn't identify any of the landmarks. The hill which the Soviet field car and the two armored personnel carriers were now descending didn't seem to be on the map. He had simply encountered too many hills and had become confused as to how far he'd strayed from his own lines.

A rocket whined past him and smashed into the slope of the nearby hill, detonating with an enormous roar. This was followed by a succession of flares, which lit up a moonscape of basins and outcroppings around him. Several tanks—all Soviet—were suddenly exposed to view.

Hahn now knew for sure that he had somehow managed to stumble into the middle of enemy lines. The Blue Force, he decided, must be ahead, and the only way to it was to plunge forward—under or through the barbed wire—and put as much distance as he could between himself and the advancing Red Force.

At the same moment as he got up from the road and began to advance, strobe lights started flashing across the length of the eastern horizon. Hahn couldn't tell what their purpose was, but their immediate effect was to temporarily blind him.

He stumbled up to the barbed wire. It cut into his jacket and scraped the skin of his hands. The cutters he tried to use weren't up to the task of severing the wire, and by the time he squeezed through the fence, he was bleeding in several places.

An antitank ditch loomed ahead, lit by a parachute flare that went off suddenly twenty yards above him.

He gained the opposite slope of the ditch and began running flat out. Followed by machine-gun fire that threw dirt into the air all around him, he raced toward what he prayed were his own forces.

After being accepted as a member of the Global Crisis Task Force, Jerry Hahn, political analyst, had expected to be trained in encoding and in contriving microdots, in managing cutouts and assuming false identities; he was ready for instruction in counterintelligence and surveillance and learning how embezzlement and blackmail could be put to good use in recruiting reluctant agents. What he was not ready for were the gymnastics, the twenty-mile runs in the morning, the weapons training, and the martial arts classes that were predicated on the theory that whatever worked should be exploited, whether it was derived from Japanese karate, tai kwon do, ju-jitsu, kung fu, or from Bruce Lee movies.

Hahn had obtained his Ph.D. in international relations at Columbia and served in Navy intelligence for two years, after which he spent a year with the Hudson Institute. But the basic training he'd received in the Navy had been nothing compared to the four-weeks-long ordeal he was going through now at the Farm.

Moreover, he'd been in his early twenties when he joined the Navy, and almost thirteen years had gone by since then. As a political analyst he had been something of a prodigy whose career had advanced him far beyond his peers. But as someone capable of handling himself in the middle of a guerrilla operation, he obviously had much to learn.

Now armed with a .32 light, Hahn was scared but determined to prove himself to William Drexell, his boss at the Task Force.

A squadron of men materialized on the crest of a slope to Hahn's left and began racing in his direction. As they zigzagged to avoid incoming shells and laser strobes, Hahn was utterly unable to tell whether they were from the Blue or Red Force.

Not knowing whether it was appropriate to run, he dropped to the ground and warily watched their progress. He soon realized that, whoever they were, there was no way they could emerge with their ranks intact.

And indeed, for all the men's evasive tactics, the strobes picked them off almost immediately, triggering the electronic sensors implanted on the backs of their helmets. For the purposes of this exercise, they were dead.

One by one, as they were killed the men dropped out of formation and trudged back in the general direction of base headquarters.

The rules of the game didn't allow Hahn to communicate with dead men, and so he waited until they were out of sight before lifting himself up from the ground and continuing in his original direction.

The man who sat in the Jeep near the Farm's perimeter didn't look as though he belonged to the twentieth century. Rather, William Drexell had the air of a Civil War general whose rough-hewn face, complete with half-smoked, unlit cigar gritted between his teeth, peered across the generations from a daguerreotype by Mathew Brady. A hammer and chisel seemed to have carved out his craggy features from very difficult material, and in actuality his tough, leathery skin had been burned by tropical sun, damaged by near Arctic cold, and touched by shrapnel.

Drexell was a man who seemed to turn up wherever in the world there was trouble. During the Second World War he'd marched with Stilwell through the Burma-India theater; in Athens, 1944, he was seen with British troops trying to suppress a Communist insurrection; not much later, in the Philippines he laid plans to destroy the *Magsaysay*; in Indochina he consorted with graduates of Saint-Cyr, who struggled in vain to hold on against the Viet Minh. In the Congo he was implicated in Lumumba's assassination; in Iran he plotted the ouster of Mossadegh; in Budapest he was seen with Imre Nagy shortly before the Soviet tanks rolled in. And when Somalia left the Soviet orbit to ally itself with the U.S. was it any coincidence that Drexell was reportedly sighted in the capital of Mogadishu?

Now he was sitting in a Jeep on a salient of the York River, which ran along one of the boundaries of the Farm.

He cursed. Stubby cigar clenched between his teeth, he turned away from the air battle across the river in which his helicopter gunships were seeking to elude the lasers being discharged by the enemy's antiaircraft guns.

With a morose expression on his face, he focused his attention on the chatter emanating from the radio. Having put himself in charge of the 3rd Division of the Blue Force, he was about to run into major trouble. A scattering of Blue positions had already been overrun, and if the quickly advancing Red Force were not soon contained, all would be lost.

"Where the fuck is the Fifth Armor?" Drexell growled at his aide, Lieutenant-Colonel Steven Cavanaugh, who was on permanent loan from the Marines.

"I don't know, sir," Cavanaugh replied tensely as he continued trying to raise contact with the 5th.

"Maybe they've been eliminated," Drexell thought aloud.

Cavanaugh confessed that he was in ignorance of the 5th's capacity to withstand the advance of the Red Force.

"Have we got any word on the Twenty-Fifth?"

The 25th was the 25th Guards Motorized Rifle Regiment. Drexell had sent them up to repel a Red infantry assault launched just a little while ago.

Cavanaugh had been in contact with the 25th only ten minutes before, but he didn't hesitate to call them again.

He was told that the 25th was holding its own but that it had been unable to dislodge the Red Force from the positions it had seized slightly to the south of a swamp code-named Scotchland.

"Get hold of General Davis," Drexell instructed.

When he was contacted, Davis was barely audible, not because of the radio's limitations but due to the din of bursting shells across the river.

"General," Drexell shouted, "you got anymore of those Sheridan tanks and maybe some of those M-60A1 tanks you're holding in reserve? I think if we draw them up to Scotchland we can break through. There's a bottle neck up there, and I'd like to put an end to it so I can make use of the Twenty-Fifth before dawn."

"I don't know what I can spare. A thrust seems to be developing over toward the Humpback. I don't want to sacrifice forces I might need to cushion it."

Humpback was a code name for a rocklike formation which enjoyed a strategic position of some importance. But Drexell doubted that any attack there by the Red Force would be more than a diversion. Even if the Humpback were lost, it would only represent a setback, not a disaster. Its importance was more a matter of General Davis' ego than anything else.

Ten minutes went by while Drexell argued, at first reasonably, then with more vehemence, in an effort to convince Davis that Drexell could make better use of the tanks. Finally Davis relented and agreed to send him half a dozen tanks, less than what he wanted, but at least it was something.

• • •

At a point midway between Scotchland and the Humpback, support units were being mobilized in the event of a sudden thrust by the Red Force.

Electronic jamming, however, was severely impeding efforts by the unit commanders to discover what was happening on the battlefield. Signals would fade in and out with infuriating frequency. For all practical purposes, brigade headquarters had become unreachable.

It was in the darkness that James Lisker functioned best. Identifiable as much by the .45 CIA deer gun he gripped in his left hand as by the scar that trailed jaggedly below his lips, he stalked with catlike alertness, both hunter and fugitive.

Up until four weeks ago, when Drexell had recalled him, he'd been in Honduras, attached to units of that country's armed forces charged with carrying out antiguerrilla operations in the north. The rain-drenched terrain by the York River was not so different from the tropical jungle that he'd just come from; both landscapes held the same capacity to ensnare the unwary in muck and tangled swampland. What was different was the shooting in Central America had been in earnest.

Drexell had assigned Lisker to the Red Force, and it had naturally fallen to him to lead this guerrilla mission. Having spent so many years in hit-and-run, cross-border operations against guerrillas, in Vietnam and Cambodia particularly, Drexell figured that Lisker deserved to see what it was like from the other side.

Lisker was a lean and angular thirty-eight years old, with eyes a chilly translucent blue and a way of looking at people that intimated that small talk would be wasted on him. An expert in tai kwon do, the Korean version of karate, he gave an impression of power just barely restrained. His air of quiet reserve only served to make him seem that much more dangerous.

While he was superbly equipped to extinguish a life or survive a jungle swarming with guerrillas, he prided himself most on his knowledge of computers and communications systems. An indication of his expertise in the latter area was the U.S. Patent Office's listing him as the inventor of an advanced encoding device that relied on the abstruse equations known as two-way functions.

While it was said he was married, he talked so seldom about his personal life that no one could be quite sure of this. At the other extreme of his activities, it was also said that he'd participated in the notorious Phoenix Program in Vietnam, assassinating suspected Vietcong sympathizers. Of course, he wouldn't admit to this either.

Despite the stories and half-rumors that clung to him, Lisker was a man who inspired trust. No one who met him ever hesitated to follow him. Tonight he had six such men with him.

As he and his men headed in the direction of the outlying Blue positions on Scotchland, the land they were traversing took a dip, descending into the swamp bordering the York River.

Barbed wire demarcated the line between the adversary positions, but Lisker's men had no difficulty cutting through it and, knee-deep in the mud, pushing forward.

The battle was drawing closer; the din of the Blues' batteries made it impossible to talk and Lisker had to use hand signals to direct the men in his command.

Gradually the earth assumed a more durable consistency and they were able to continue on with greater speed. To their right was the York River, and to their left, half a mile away at two o'clock, T-55 and T-62

Soviet-manufactured tanks were rolling steadily toward Blue artillery installations. BMP's, with 73mm guns, were following right behind. Lasers slashed through the night and flares popped continuously. With the enormous amount of smoke, the landscape took on a spectral appearance.

In the meantime, a brigade of Blue infantry was making its way through a copse of pines a little to the left. Lisker had his men advance until they were within range of the enemy, but hidden by brush. Then he ordered them to wait until they were sure of their targets. He assumed, by the adversaries' number and position, that they must be detached from the 25th Rifle Guards.

It was 22:35 hours when Lisker gave the order to open fire.

As he had guessed, the men he was ambushing were in fact part of the 25th. What he did not know was that he was acquainted with one of them, a man named Zoccola.

Whenever a laser beam would slash through the darkness in John Zoccola's direction he somehow managed not to be there. Tracer bullets lit through the air, targeted right on him, but they'd always end up hitting the brush through which he raced.

John Zoccola wasn't short or noticeably thin, but there was something about him that reminded people of a jockey. He moved fluidly, quickly; you had the feeling he could make himself invisible if the urge came over him. Further, if you looked carefully into his eyes, you would note cunning there. Although you'd do better than to trust his smile, he wasn't consciously deceptive. He was simply mercuvial by nature, outgoing one minute, unresponsive the next.

No one knew this better than the women who became involved with him. Once they fell in love with him, they never seemed able to disentangle themselves. Those beguiled by Zoccola's changeable nature included two former wives.

A man of action, John Zoccola knew he could fit in anywhere, that he was as capable of handling a military maneuver in the swamps of Virginia as he was bidding up the price of gold and treasury futures on the Comex, which was, in fact, what he once did in the days when his youthful energy directed him to acquire vast amounts of capital. And if he later were to don a three-piece suit with a gold watch chain leaking from his vest pocket, and conclude deals for international loans amid opulent settings, with Matisses and Vuillards smiling down on him, why, it was only another scene in his lifetime charade.

He wished he could speed up now. The faraway fighting was reaching a fevered pitch, and it was frustrating having to proceed at the lugubrious pace of the recon patrol. Its orders were to probe enemy positions, and this was not done easily or quickly when there was no evidence available as to where the enemy was.

All at once that evidence was provided in great abundance.

The brush and dead trees that flanked the patrol on its left came alive with the light of penetrating lasers. Everywhere around him Zoccola could hear the sharp buzz of electronic wizardry as the beacons in their helmets were set off. Of the sixteen men, eight were struck immediately and began to retire from the field of battle.

The rest, including Zoccola, dropped down and began returning the fire. But the vegetation was too thick and lent the adversary force all the cover it needed. When the next assault came, it originated from another point, catching the tattered patrol by surprise.

"Goddamn son of a bitch," one of the Blue officers cried after a laser had found him. He angrily got to his feet and hurled his buzzing helmet into the mud.

"We've got to move out or we'll be fucked!" a second officer shouted and immediately began to do just that.

An instant later he and those who elected to follow him were also hit.

Those, like Zoccola, who remained sprawled on the ground, found themselves surrounded. There was nothing to do but surrender.

When he looked up and saw that it was Lisker who'd organized the ambush, he shook his head and muttered, "I should have known."

There, caught in the flickering light of battle, was James Lisker. With his dark, cropped hair and his bony, heavily shadowed features, he looked almost skeletal.

Lisker gave Zoccola no sign of recognition and when he trained his .45 on him, Zoccola understood that he was expected to drop his own PK Walther. After he reluctantly complied, Lisker allowed the shadow of a smile. "That's better," he said quietly.

It was then that they heard the motor of an approaching vehicle. Ambushers, prisoners, and the "killed" alike turned to see whose it was.

A lone Jeep bearing Blue Force markings entered the clearing. Lisker was about to have his men open fire when he noticed Drexell sitting up next to the driver. He realized Drexell was not about to drive through the middle of a war game on his own unless it involved some matter of greater urgency.

The Jeep stopped near the combatants, and Drexell jumped down. Seeing Lisker and Zoccola together, he gave a satisfied nod. "Two in one shot," he said, then added abruptly, "We have a problem."

"*We* do?" Zoccola asked. He thought he was the one with the problem.

Without replying directly, Drexell turned to Lisker. "You think you can handle a little trip tonight?"

"Where to?"

"Morocco."

"When do I leave?"

"As soon as I find Hahn," said Drexell. "No telling what the fuck happened to him. We haven't had radio contact with him since twenty-one hundred hours."

Hahn was four miles southeast of his colleagues. Not quite certain where he was, he surmised correctly that he was close to Humpback.

He continued in the same direction, hoping it would bring him into contact with his own forces. He forded a small stream that wasn't identified on either of the maps he carried, and after cutting through a tangle of waist-high barbed wire, found himself in a densely wooded area.

With no other point of orientation, he headed toward the smoke and the shooting. He didn't hear, until it was too late, the sound of footsteps to his rear.

"Halt!"

He stopped dead.

"Identify yourself."

"Tidewater Indigo," he said, using the prearranged code.

There was silence. He concluded that he'd strayed into Red Force territory and now waited to be told that he'd been taken prisoner.

The other soldier stepped forward, his gun lowered. "You lucky bastard, you've come home," he said.

3

At eleven in the morning, only slightly the worse for wear, three members of the Global Crisis Task Force assembled at their temporary headquarters on the sixth floor of the State Department building to discuss the disappearance of the American satellite over Morocco. This was only the fifth time that the Task Force had officially come together since its inception. Its members, however, had met informally several times in the previous months in order to better familiarize themselves with Triad's procedures—and with one another.

Present at this meeting were William Drexell, John Zoccola, and Jerry Hahn. Also present was Drexell's aide, Lieutenant-Colonel Cavanaugh. Lisker, the only member missing, was in Morocco, having arrived there earlier that morning.

They convened in a windowless, minimally furnished conference room at their temporary quarters. The room's only points of interest were the situation maps strung across every wall.

Drexell chose a seat for himself at the head of the table. Cavanaugh, armed with all the documents relevant to the Moroccan affair, took a chair on his right. The other two sat on either side of the conference table.

There was no ignoring Drexell when he spoke. His distinctively hoarse voice had an authority gained from innumerable cold war campaigns. Now he began by giving them all a short refresher on the region of Africa that compelled their interest.

The area was known as the Maghreb. Extending from Morocco in the west to Tunisia, Libya, and Algeria in the east, it had been, until the midfifties, dominated by the French (with the exception of Libya, where the Italians had held sway). In contrast to the bloody upheaval that accompanied the liberation of Algeria from French control, Morocco, Tunisia, and Libya had all gained their independence with a minimum of turbulence.

While Morocco and Tunisia were currently entrenched in the Western camp, advocating relatively liberal policies, Algeria had swung to a course that was socialist and more favorably disposed toward the Soviets. But none of these three nations was as radical or as erratic as Libya under the rule of Colonel Muammar al-Qaddafi.

Drexell interrupted his comments to get up and move to one of the large, strategy maps covering part of the wall to his left. It was a detailed topographical map built up from a series of overlapping high-resolution photographs taken by a surveillance satellite two months previously.

Cavanaugh handed him a pointer, and he touched the map with it. The pointer cast a shadow that extended from Tripoli on the northern coast of Libya all the way into the southern depths of the Algerian desert. Before Drexell spoke, however, Zoccola, with his exhaustive knowledge of the world's natural resources, knew immediately that this swath of desert contained little to interest anyone.

"Until this May, the United States carried out routine satellite reconnaissance of this terrain," Drexell began. "At that time there was no reason to expect significant problems from Libya or any other part of the Maghreb. As you know, most of our reconnaissance efforts were directed toward the sub-Sahara region where we detected renewed but limited activity on the part of the Polisario insurgents in Morocco."

Drexell now moved his pointer to a place in Libya slightly to the left of Tripoli and tapped it twice against a dark patch that looked like nothing so much as a bug that had gotten squashed as it tried to scramble across the 1-to-12,000 scale map.

"The last group of photographs relayed to us by the satellite differed significantly from the earlier ones. The difference was this darkened area. To get a better handle on what was going on, we reprogrammed the satellite camera for much greater detail."

He signaled to his aide, who carefully wheeled out a mobile board to which were pinned several of the more detailed photographs. They showed an encampment of hundreds of white tents occupied by what appeared to be nomadic Bedouin, their heads and faces swathed in djbellas. Heightening the impression of routine desert life were a number of camels tethered nearby.

"What struck us first was that this particular encampment was far larger than what you usually find in the area. We've done estimates which indicate that, given the number and size of the tents, in excess of fifteen hundred people could be accommodated in the encampment. But that's only part of the story.''

Drexell now moved the pointer to another set of photographs pinned at the right of the board.

"Looking closely at these,'' Drexell continued, "you might be reminded of an unoccupied house where all the furniture is covered with sheets.''

The others saw how apt the analogy was; the photographs disclosed any number of strange geometrical shapes—a rounded object here, a cube there, a trapezoid just beyond it—whose identities were disguised by vast expanses of canvaslike material.

"Camouflaged military hardware,'' concluded Hahn.

"That was what our photo boys thought,'' Drexell agreed. "But the bird we have in orbit above Libya lacks the infrared sensor equipment we needed to determine what we really had. And that's why we tried to launch Secsat DV-2. Or one of the reasons. We also wanted to use the new satellite to determine the capability of the Libyans' desert missile installation, but I'll discuss that in a minute. As you know, right after the firing for geosynchronous orbit, communications went down between the facilities here and our linkup in Morocco. The interruption lasted for less than a minute —long enough to keep us from getting any data on why it disappeared.''

"What's being done now?'' Hahn asked.

"We've been in contact with MILINET in the last twenty-four hours, but we've received no report of anything untoward occurring to any of our other satellites. All systems appear to be operating normally.''

MILINET was the Defense Department's elaborate computer network, much of which was linked to commercial satellites and to such multipurpose computers as those at MIT, CalTech, NATO headquarters in Brussels, and, of course, at the Pentagon itself. The network had the highest surveillance usefulness, as virtually all of the data relayed by military satellites found its way into MILINET.

"What we're worried about is that the Soviets have perfected some kind of high-energy laser weapon—either a chemical laser with a ten-megawatt output or a particle beam weapon. But of course we're talking about a highly speculative *Star Wars* type invention, and it isn't really the sort of possibility I'm really looking for here."

"What about something launched from the ground?" Zoccola asked, seeing Drexell's point.

"An interesting possibility," Drexell admitted. "But we have no evidence of such a launch from within Soviet territory. And unfortunately, our other North African satellite was too far away from the Libyan base to help us detect any activity there."

Drexell's pointer was now indicating a black cross approximately a thousand kilometers south of Tripoli, Libya, right in the middle of the Sahara. "Some years back an independent East German company, Orbital Transport und Raketen Aktiengesellschaft, ORTAG for short, built a launch site here for the Libyan government. ORTAG was manufacturing what you might call bargain basement spacecraft. A few years ago I heard they were asking thirty million for an Atlas-Centaur class booster, and a mere seventeen and a half mil for a Delta class. In the last several months we've had reports, so far unverified, that the Germans are no longer in charge of the launch base, either that or else they're taking orders directly from the Libyans. The most obvious hypothesis we're considering is, of course, that a weapon might have been launched from this base by the Libyan government."

After a moment during which he gave the men of the Task Force a chance to absorb the somber implications of his last statement, Drexell sat down and continued speaking from his seat at the head of the table.

"I'm not at all sure how we go ahead on this thing," Hahn said with some anxiousness.

"First off," Drexell said in his gravelly voice, "each of us is going to have to risk his ass surveilling everything going down in that region right now. Your major job, Jerry, will be to find out what's going on on the Tunisian-Libyan border. If somebody is willing to shoot our bird out of the sky, we have to assume that what they're trying to divert our attention from is mighty important."

It was obvious to Hahn that he had been chosen for this particular task because of his political acumen and his personal familiarity with the area. In a few moments Drexell had filled him in completely on where and how and by what time to reconnoiter the Tunisian situation —both in terms of current political climate and vis-à-vis the Libyan border. "When you leave Tunis for the interior," Drexell finished in a warning voice, "you ought to prepare yourself for a real survival situation."

Wanting to avoid discussion of the harrowing circumstances he might have to face, Hahn changed the focus of the discussion. "Do you think the Russians are involved?" he asked.

"My feeling is that, yes, there has to be Soviet involvement. They're the only ones who would have the training to take out our bird like that. And while neither Algeria nor Libya is a Russian satellite, their interests and the Soviets' coincide enough that I'm sure Libya would be more than happy to destabilize Tunisia and Morocco, the two pro-Western states in the area, even without Moscow's backing. But what's happening in North Africa—and this includes the Polisario's starting up again with Morocco—seems to be orchestrated from one source, and the Russians are the only ones with the capability for putting fingers in so many pies.

"What we're most concerned about, of course," he continued emphatically, "is that if the Soviets destabilize North Africa, they get closer to control of the Mediterranean. And if they get that, they can begin to neutralize Western Europe."

Drexell turned to Zoccola on his right. "I'd like you to do a different sort of job, John. See if you can ferret out a man, a GRU officer we've code-named Mr. Clean who works for Soviet army intelligence. It seems to me that with your diplomatic finesse—as well as your innate charms," Drexell added with friendly sarcasm, "that you can shop him easily enough. His profile indicates that he can be bought, and I don't doubt you have a way with greedy men.

"I'll get you all the documentation on him you'll need," Drexell continued. "We know he's somewhere in the Maghreb, shuttling back and forth between Tripoli and Algiers. We also know he's been meeting with Polisario insurgents in the Western Sahara. But we're not sure what the ultimate aim of all his peregrinations might be."

"How hard will he be to find?" Zoccola asked.

"I don't think it should be too difficult. He poses as a trade representative, some sort of businessman from the Eastern bloc, and he's doing nothing to make himself inconspicuous. I'll see that you have the reading material on him before you start out for the airport tonight."

Changing to a more businesslike tone, Drexell said to Cavanaugh, "Patch in Mr. Lisker on line eight, please."

After a few minutes during which Zoccola and Hahn were able to inquire in more detail about their respective missions, the phone emitted an impatient buzz, confirming that the hookup to El Jadida had been secured.

"We're patched in, sir," Cavanaugh announced.

"Excellent. Put him on conference."

Suddenly Lisker's voice blared unintelligibly from the two phone speakers.

"Turn down the volume," Drexell snapped. To Lisker he said, "Jim, how are you doing?"

"Getting along, sir."

"We've got Hahn and Zoccola at this end. Ready when you are."

"Tell me what's new first," Lisker asked.

"Nothing at all. MILINET's negative."

"Too bad. Only one thing of interest here. But it's a big one."

"We're listening, Jim."

"The man in charge of El Jadida turned up dead last night."

"Shobokshi?"

"That's right. Skull crushed in. A messy job, I'm told. He'd supposedly called in sick to the ground station twenty-four hours previously. But I can't find out who took the call. It's possible that someone—maybe the murderer—called in sick for him."

"What happened to his replacement—?" here Drexell's enviable memory deserted him and he was forced to consult his notes "—this Ibrahim Brega guy Ross was talking to from Mission Control."

"I can't locate Brega or even find anyone who admits knowing him. The story I've been told is that he was called in at the last minute to see that everything worked smoothly on the apogee motor firing maneuver."

"On whose authority?"

"On the authority of some minister in Rabat. Ordinarily a high-level decision like that would have to be okayed by our own security adviser at El Jadida, but he was evidently preoccupied at the time."

"By what?"

"Whom. A young woman. He's now on his way home—sacked."

"And what about the minister?"

"I haven't been able to figure out which minister it was."

Drexell didn't respond for a moment. "And Brega's disappeared?" he finally asked coldly. "That's what you're saying?"

"Into thin air. Just like our satellite."

4

JULY 21
OVER LIBYA

On July 21, a hot cloudless day that exactly resembled the many days before it, two highly maneuverable F-16A's took off from a secret U.S.-Egyptian airbase less than 300 miles west of the Egyptian-Libyan border, and swept across the invisible demarcation line that separated the two countries.

This violation of Libyan airspace was quickly registered by radar and reported to the air ministry in Tripoli. The border with Egypt had seldom been a peaceful one—there were estimated to be close to 100,000 Egyptian troops deployed along it—and both sides monitored it as closely as possible given the sheer length of the border and the vastness of the surrounding terrain.

The two F-16A's bore no markings. However, they were clearly of U.S. manufacture, and this far into Libyan airspace, there could be no question of navigational error. They quickly climbed to close their service ceiling of 60,000 feet, maintaining a speed of Mach 1, only slightly more than half their maximum.

Within eight minutes two MiG-21F's rose into the air from a base just inside Libya. Their orders were to intercept the F-16's and shoot the American aircraft down.

Twelve minutes after the violation was first recorded, two SA-4 missiles were fired from a mobile ground launcher. Primarily used against long-range, high-flying aircraft, they were an integral part of the new Soviet-designed heavy battlefield missile system installed in the early 1980s.

It would be less than a minute before the advanced pulse-doppler radar, situated in the nose cones of the F-16's, would register the approach of the missiles.

In the meantime J. C. Richards, pilot of one of the American craft, was carrying on a conversation with his colleague, Lew Sam Jones, whose plane was maintaining a course almost parallel to his.

"Lots of desert out there, hey? Over."

"Sand, sand, and more sand, J. C. Looks like we're golden. Over."

"Roger, Sampson-Three. Should be out of here by cocktail hour. Over."

"I can't read you, Ranger-One, what was that again? Over."

"Oh, no, wait a minute now. We've got something on radar. You see it, Sampson-Three? Over."

"I see it all right. Let's move out of their way. Over."

In tandem the two pilots veered their jets sharply to the southeast, accelerating simultaneously to a speed of Mach 1.6 and leaving the SA-4s far behind. In moments, the missiles detonated harmlessly in the air, and from their reclining Escapac seats, Richards and Sam

Jones watched them erupting into bright orange balls of fire.

The U.S. aircraft resumed their northwesterly flight toward the Tunisian border. However, as the F-16's approached Tamassah, approximately 200 miles north of the Libyan-Chad border, additional MiG-21's with AA-2 Atoll IR-homing missiles, were put into the air.

One of the MiG's, climbing to an altitude of 50,000 feet, 9,000 below its service ceiling, materialized off to the right of the two F-16's. It banked sharply, firing the 30mm NR gun located under its fuselage prior to launching the first of the two Atoll (K-13) missiles on its wing pylons.

Neither the rounds from the NR gun nor the missile succeeded in hitting Richards's F-16. With his sidestick controllers, the endangered pilot maneuvered his craft down and away from the fire, then brought it into a position suitable for retaliatory action. With its maximum weapon load, the F-16 had an attack radius of 120 miles; now the MiG and the F-16's were within seven miles of one another.

An intricate choreography of air power was displayed in the next half minute as all three jets sought more favorable situations. A second MiG, now at an altitude of 28,000 feet and climbing, appeared off to the northeast, still a speck of gray in the vast blue sky.

Suddenly Sam Jones triggered off one of his wingtip AIM-9L Sidewinder missiles. It cut a swath across the horizon and impacted precisely on target, instantly obliterating the MiG.

At this point in the engagement the following transmission, which was recorded by Libyan intelligence services and was later released to the international wire services, took place between the two pilots of the F-16's.

Pilot 1: Bearing due north. Over.

Pilot 2: Roger. Hold steady at (unintelligible).

Pilot 1: Roger. Squawk Whiskey-one, zero-three, zero-five, low. Do you read me?

Pilot 2: Loud and clear. Inbound Echo-Sierra. I have a DME fix of eighty-five and closing with a radial of seventy-two degrees. Over.

Pilot 1: I can see it now. DME arc interception at eighty-eight degrees. Over.

Pilot 2: Affirmative. Going into (unintelligible).

Pilot 1: Track at forty-forty. Over.

Pilot 2: Out of it now. Wait, I'm getting something on the (unintelligible). Inbound Echo-Sierra. Have you got a DME fix for that?

Pilot 1: Affirmative. Hundred and sixteen nautical and a radial of ninety-one. Closing from the west-southwest. Over.

Pilot 2: Holding true at one hundred sixty-two. Over.

Pilot 1: Foxtrot Lima Whiskey at one-two, one-two. Do you read me?

Pilot 2: She's right off to my left. Pulling up and crossing—

The transmission ended abruptly when the second of two heat-seeking missiles launched from the ground struck an underwing tank of Jones's F-16, and a thunderous explosion ripped the jet in two. The two halves careened the tens of thousands of feet down, trailing smoke all the way to the empty desert floor.

The second F-16 was more fortunate. It succeeded in outdistancing the land-to-air missiles and the pursuing MiG's, and within twenty minutes it was cruising over its designated target area—a forbidding stretch of desolate terrain, characterized by treacherous mountain ridges and the wastes of a desert known to its inhabitants as Al Hammadah.

When Richards arrived over the desert of Al Hammadah—some forty miles from the Tunisian border—he had little idea of what to expect. He'd been given orders only to conduct a routine surveillance, which was to be supplemented by photographs automatically taken by special radio-activated camera equipment.

Richards was advised to be on the lookout for signs of military activity, open or concealed, but so far he could see nothing out of the ordinary. No Jeeps, no tanks, no camouflaged airfield. He was beginning to wonder whether the mission had been worth the loss of a highly trained pilot and a $40 million airplane when he directed the F-16 farther north and finally saw something of interest. It didn't seem military in nature, but it sure astonished the hell out of J. C. Richards, who, being Texan, was not easily impressed.

Twenty thousand feet below him was a meandering desert highway, redder in color than the surrounding dunes and rock formations, and for miles and miles along this road, proceeding at a slow but inexorable pace, was a caravan of thousands of people. Flying by a second time, Richards thought that if there was one thing you never expected to see in the desert of Libya, a huge country with a population barely exceeding two million, it was a good segment of that population migrating north toward neighboring Tunisia.

After the second pass, the F-16 banked to the left and began traveling northeast, in the direction the road was taking. In moments Richards had crossed into Tunisian airspace.

Less than an hour later he was bringing the jet down on the deck of the *Nimitz*, one of the U.S.'s principal aircraft carriers in the Mediterranean-based Sixth Fleet.

He was not allowed time to change but was handed a cup of coffee and escorted immediately into the wardroom for a preliminary debriefing.

Three men, two high-ranking Naval officers and a third in civilian dress, were waiting expectantly for him. The two officers identified themselves as Rear Admiral Martin Holloway and Captain Louis Patterson. The Admiral was going gray, and the captain was going bald, and from what Richards could tell, they were both in their early sixties. The third man was some years younger, not exactly handsome but with unforgettable features—especially the deepset eyes and sharp nose that looked as if it had once been broken. Richards sensed the man's tenseness immediately; he sat poised on the edge of his chair as though he expected to be called away on an emergency at any moment. He also had a thin, almost invisible wire winding down from his ear into some sort of radio device in his pocket. Here, Richards thought, was a man with powerful connections.

The civilian announced that his name was James Lisker. That was all. No rank, no way of figuring out who he represented. Intuitively Richards assumed he was CIA.

"How are you feeling?" Admiral Holloway asked, providing the civilities before starting in on more important matters.

"Not too terrific, sir. Those scum, if you'll excuse the expression, they got one of my friends." Richards spoke in a quiet drawl that underlined the plain feeling behind his words.

"I know, and I'm sorry. Now, can you tell us exactly what happened?" Holloway kept his voice sympathetic and subtly neutral at the same time.

"All I can figure is that he was too slow. I don't know why he didn't get out of the way of that SAM quicker. We were talking just before it hit him. We had it on our radar, we had it spotted. There didn't seem to be no problem, just a matter of dodging it, when all of a sudden, bam, nothing, he's gone."

"Thank you, Colonel," Holloway said. Then he turned to Lisker. "Well, there's no doubt going to be flack on this. The President will have to make a statement in a few hours, don't you think?"

For the first time, Lisker spoke at length. He had an impressive voice, and it struck Richards that he would make a great radio announcer, the kind whose voice you hear late at night, deep, resonant, and lonely as all hell. "I think contingency plans have been arranged," he assured the Admiral. "We were aware of the risks, and we're fully prepared to take the heat." Frowning, he added, "Now, let's see whether it was worth the trouble." Turning to the pilot he asked him to describe what he saw in the desert.

"I didn't see anything but desert and sky until I got over Al Hammadah—"

"Show us on this, Colonel," Lisker interrupted, indicating a detailed topographical map of Libya, large as a blanket, that spilled over the gray metal table in the center of the room. Richards studied it for a while, then put the tip of his ring finger in the appropriate place. "There."

"And what did you see?"

"I saw five, six hundred people, maybe a thousand; it's hard to say. They were walking along a road. Some had camels, and there were some Jeeps and a number of open-backed trucks."

"Military?" Lisker asked.

"You'll have to check the photos, but from my vantage it didn't look like it. No evidence of guns, no tanks, nothing that would make you think you were dealing with an army. Besides, those people sure as hell didn't look like an army. Looked like a lot of damn peasants to me."

"And all they were doing was walking along this road?" Holloway asked indignantly. It was clear to Richards that the Admiral thought they had lost a man and a fine piece of hardware just to see a thousand peasants marching through the Libyan desert.

"That's right."

"And where," Lisker asked, "did they appear to be heading?"

"Well, in my opinion, they were heading right into Tunisia."

The three men behind the table exchanged somber looks. They had altogether forgotten the presence of J. C. Richards.

Excerpt from Presidential News Conference, July 22nd 1986.

The President: Before taking any questions, I would like to make a brief opening statement.

Yesterday, at approximately 3:30 p.m. local time, 9:30 in the morning eastern time, a U.S. Naval aircraft was shot down by a Libyan missile. The pilot of that aircraft is presumed to have been lost. Although Tripoli radio is reporting that a second aircraft was also downed we firmly deny that any such event occurred. There was no second aircraft involved in the incident. As you may already know, the incident in question occurred near Tunisian territory. From time to time, in cooperation with the Tunisian authorities, we have sponsored aerial and naval exercises. While we don't yet have all the facts, we are reasonably certain that the aircraft strayed into Libyan territory. We regret the error and our interests section in the Swiss embassy has conveyed its regrets to Mr. Qaddafi. We are still investigating the circumstances in the matter and when we know more we'll be sure to let you know. Now I will take questions.

Q: Mr. President?

A: You, right in front.

Q. Dan Riley, Detroit *Free-Press*. The Libyans are claiming that the two planes involved in the incident were flying from Egypt and not from Tunisia.

A: The Libyans have claimed many things. That report is simply not true. Yes, Miss Davis?

Q: Is it true that Qaddafi has rejected your apology?

A: I understand that to be the case, yes. Over in the back there.

Q: Lou Simonini, L.A. *Times*. Mr. President, there have been rumors in the last few days that one of our spy satellites has been lost in space and might possibly have been shot down. And further, that there might have been a link between the incident yesterday over Libyan territory and the downing of that satellite.

A: What's the question?

(Laughter.)

Q: Is there any truth to these rumors and was the overflight intended as a reconnaissance mission?

A: As far as I know there is no substance to these rumors. Mr. Winthrop.

Q: For years now the U.S. has regarded the Libyans as belligerents, with Qaddafi fostering terrorism around the world and sending troops to Chad and Uganda in support of dictators like Idi Amin. Does the incident yesterday mark a policy change? Are we going to start getting tough with Qaddafi?

A: Like my predecessors in this office, I am seriously concerned with the manner in which Mr. Qaddafi has been stirring up trouble at every opportunity. We regard him quite frankly as a threat to peace. But we are not aiming to overthrow his regime, as he sometimes charges, nor are we attempting to isolate him. If he cares to behave as a member of a civilized community of nations then he will be treated as such. So in answer to your question, no, what happened yesterday was an isolated, and regrettable, incident and it does not mark any departure from previous policy positions that we have taken in regard to Libya. Down in front.

Q: Franklin Trent, Philadelphia *Inquirer*. Last week's unemployment statistics show a continued rise in spite of your new economic program. Do you see this as a setback to that program?

A: Well, let me say I'm glad to get off the subject of Libya . . .

(Laughter.)

Excerpt ends.

5

Except for the White House passes, which hung from chains around their necks, the two men seated in the Situation Room in the west wing had little in common. Jeffrey Schelling, the Secretary of State, seemed embarrassed by the obligatory identification required by the Secret Service and had tucked his discreetly into his jacket pocket. Not William Drexell, who let it dangle clumsily across his chest, indifferent to its presence.

Sitting across from each other at the large table, the two men were a study in contrasts. Schelling, a man in his midfifties with a passion for athletics and sailing, was eminently photogenic, radiating good health and a sense of command. He not only looked as though he had just emerged from the pages of *Town & Country* magazine, he actually had. He and his wife, a woman of well-preserved beauty, graceful manners, and a sizable inheritance, had recently been featured in the magazine, photographed on their Virginia estate in the company of their children, their horses, and their aging black retainers.

By contrast, Drexell presented a gruff, slightly rumpled appearance that made him seem out of place in such overly decorous circumstances as these. Somewhat squat and muscular, he had the eye-drooping ease of a cagy poker player. Holding a long-ashed cigar between his stubby fingers, he was now a more contemporary version of a Civil War general. He didn't speak to the other man in the room but occasionally annoyed Schelling by exhaling pungent clouds of acrid smoke into the air.

When the President entered, followed by Morse Peckum, his chief of staff, his two visitors stood to greet him.

Of an ordinary night, the President was as likely as not to pull up a chair and conduct long, rambling disquisitions on the state of the world or else launch into extended reminiscences from his boyhood. Tonight, however, he was brusque and to the point, perhaps seeing that he might now have to face the first real international crisis of his administration. In office almost exactly a year and six months, Creighton Turner apparently that he'd hoped somehow to make it through four years without having to commit himself to any course of action that could not be repudiated or cancelled out the next day. The problem was less that Turner had a vacillating personality than that he sometimes seemed afraid of the awesome responsibilities of the office.

The President and his chief of staff took chairs opposite the visitors. Turner began immediately: "I'm looking for two things from you gentlemen tonight. First off, Jeffrey, I want you to tell me what we have on the situation in the Kremlin at this hour. Then I want to be briefed as to what in hell is going on in North Africa.

CIA keeps sending me these alarming reports, and frankly they've got me worried. That's your department, William."

Schelling gave Drexell a withering glance. Schelling had neither approved of the establishment of the Task Force nor condoned the President's reliance on it. It was only to appease the President that he had assented to the Task Force's temporary presence within State's offices at Foggy Bottom. Although he had made Drexell's acquaintance several years before, he had never till now had the opportunity to directly express his instinctive distaste for him.

"I beg your pardon, Mr. President, but I wonder why you haven't invited Tom or Marty to join us."

Schelling was referring to Thomas Kriendler, the National Security Advisor, and to Martin Rhiel, the Secretary of Defense.

"Don't worry, Jeffrey, they'll be kept informed. We certainly don't want to keep them in the dark."

But that was exactly what he was doing, Drexell realized. It was the President's style. The only reason Schelling was here was to create a facade of unity in foreign policy, and to accomplish that, Schelling couldn't very well be left out—not if he was going to communicate their position to America's allies.

Schelling slumped back, resigned but far from defeated.

"I'm afraid I have nothing new on the events in the Kremlin," the Secretary of State said. "The Soviet watch desk is working on a round-the-clock basis, but we keep coming up with the same information. Kirilenko seems to be out. Now, whether that's because he's ill, as the Tass bulletins say, or because he's been ousted, we don't know. We have indications that Alexei Kadiyev has been named by the Politburo as First Secretary of the Communist Party.''

The President looked disappointed. None of this was new to him. As had been the case for the past seventy-two hours, there was still no telling who was running the show.

''What do we have on Kadiyev?''

''For a brief time Kadiyev was the Soviet negotiator on arms limitations in Geneva, that was back in 'eighty, 'eighty-one. Prior to that he served as ambassador to West Germany and Brazil. He's in his late fifties, which of course is quite young to have reached the pinnacle of Soviet leadership. One could say his rise has been meteoric if, in fact, he has been made First Secretary.''

''But what is he—hawk? dove?''

Drexell felt his usual annoyance at the President's need to define things in such black-and-white terms. What was the difference between a hawk or dove inside the Kremlin anyhow? Was the man who pushed the button a hawk and was the man who preached detente and sent troops into Czechoslovakia and Afghanistan a dove?

Drexell's rough voice filled the Situation Room. ''There's no way to give Kadiyev an easy label. He's nowhere as cosmopolitan or as familiar with the West as Andropov was. But he *is* reputed to be intelligent and shrewd, even open-minded. He likes cognac, not vodka, and like Brezhnev he has a tendency to smoke too much —Marlboros, specifically. His primary support comes from the army.''

Drexell's words about the Soviet army added weight, given the events of the past few years. Yuri Andropov, former head of the KGB, had assumed the leadership of the Communist Party right after Leonid Brezhnev's death at the age of 75, but he'd failed to retain his position, Western analysts believed, because he'd been unable to placate the military, whose influence over the regime was more powerful than ever.

Schelling, however, was not inclined to trust Drexell's judgment. "Nobody I've spoken to on the watch desk believes that the Red Army's pushing Kadiyev or making any other moves for power. I don't know where you're getting your information from."

"The most obvious indication," Drexell replied, "will be heightened military activity by the Russians, probably in the southern Mediterranean."

"Are you saying that the Politburo is ready to stir up trouble just to placate their generals?" Schelling was sounding increasingly bombastic as he realized his lack of access to the sort of information Drexell was privy to.

"I think that's an accurate assessment," Drexell replied curtly.

"What *is* the present situation in the Mediterranean?" the President asked.

"There's no question, sir, that their Black Sea Fleet is being deployed in a significant way east of the Strait of Gibraltar. Our recon satellites have turned up evidence that several vessels—in addition to the ones they've already sent in—are leaving from bases in Sevastopol, Nikolaev, and Odessa. There are a total of eighty-eight large surface ships either in the Mediterranean or on their way. Accompanying these vessels, the Russians also have from ten to fifteen subs, about half estimated to be nuclear powered, and anywhere from eighty to one hundred bombers. And of course there are also the large number of support craft for supplies and repairs at sea."

"What's the proportional increase?"

"A few weeks ago, on June thirtieth, there were only forty-two vessels, including support craft, in the Mediterranean. That means we've had an increase of more than one hundred percent in a period of twenty-three days.''

"That kind of buildup,'' the President said, "means one of two things. It's either a signal, a political gesture for the benefit of the Red Army, or else the Soviets have a definite military objective in mind. I am unable to believe that it's the latter. It's been my experience that the Soviets act only when there's a window of vulnerability. They saw opportunities in Afghanistan, Angola, and Ethiopia and they took them. But they don't advance on a target unless that opportunity exists. Frankly, I don't see any exploitable opportunities for them at present in the Mediterranean.''

"Try Libya,'' Drexell stated flatly. "Libya will provide them with the opportunity, possibly by invading Tunisia.''

Drexell knew he was jumping the gun here; the Task Force had just arrived in North Africa and had yet to discover hard evidence of Soviet interference.

Schelling sensed that Drexell might not have the facts to back up his claims. He said smoothly, "We have no evidence that anything critical will happen between Libya and Tunisia, at least not in the next few months.''

"You've seen the recon photos,'' Drexell replied shortly.

"We've seen them,'' the President said, suddenly impatient, "but for the moment I think Jeffrey's right. We'll wait twenty-four to forty-eight hours, longer if necessary. By then the dust may have settled at the Kremlin. Meanwhile, we're sending a strong signal to the Soviets by moving the Sixth Fleet toward North Africa. I suggest we all get ourselves a good night's sleep, gentlemen, and see what the morning brings.''

6

It was possible to detect the faint rumble of the train
long before it could be seen. This early in the morning,
the desert below the southern border of Morocco was
ordinarily free of sound save for the mournful voice of
the wind creating patterns in the dunes. But the schedule
of the express from Nouadhibou had recently been
changed, and it now started its run before dawn, both to
escape the scorching heat of the desert sun and to avoid
guerrilla attack by using the cover of early-morning
darkness.

There hadn't been a guerrilla attack since the previous
December, just before the United Nations truce had
gone into effect. But rumors had been circulating
through high Moroccan government circles that the Polisario were now preparing another campaign, this time
bolstered by more advanced weaponry supplied them by
their Soviet and Algerian sponsors.

Gradually the train came into view. At first a speck
of black, belching white steam into a slate-gray sky, it

revealed itself little by little as an engine followed by a series of twenty phosphorus-loaded cars. As it continued north along the desert floor, it picked up speed. Less than forty miles from the seacoast, this area was regarded as especially dangerous, harboring as it did the camps of hundreds of insurgent soldiers.

On board was a large contingent of Moroccan soldiers, bristling with M-16's and machine guns. Positioned in cars at both the front and rear of the train, they observed the passing landscape with apprehension, straining for any sign of the enemy in the predawn darkness. But the desert continued to yield no sign of human life.

To the east, a band of amber light was beginning to brighten at the horizon. If any attack was to come, it would happen within the next several minutes, for the enemy only acted under cover of darkness.

The train left the flat desert to slowly wind its way through a gorge and then up into a semimountainous area.

At 5:28, approximately four hours out of Nouadhibou, the engineer, peering out of his cabin, noticed what appeared to be a series of thin wires lying taut over the rails up ahead. Not sure whether he was seeing correctly in the dim light, he nevertheless moved by instinct and, with a violent motion, yanked down on the cord connected to the emergency brake.

The momentum of the engine was too great to bring the train to a halt before reaching the wires. As soon as the locomotive's front wheels touched them, they triggered a powerful plastic explosive which set off a series of other charges, one immediately after the other.

Initially, the sound of the continuing detonations was somewhat muffled by the clatter of the wheels on the tracks, but even to the soldiers all the way at the rear of the train there was no mistaking the dread import of the explosive sounds.

The engine shuddered, heaving back and forth even as it was propelled by the force of the explosion half into the air. A ball of flame erupted in the cabin, tearing its machinery to shreds and exploding hundreds of metal fragments off in all directions. For an instant the contorted form of one of the engineers tumbled clumsily in the air, his face obscenely charred, his torso riddled with shards of the locomotive he'd only moments before been attempting to stop. Carried by its momentum the locomotive momentarily rocked back to solid ground, then what was left of it slewed wildly off the tracks and into a desert ravine, taking with it several cars that banged clamorously against one another. Finally coming to a near halt, the configuration of engine and cars teetered to the side for a moment before collapsing in an immense smoke heap.

Not all the soldiers trapped in the cars behind the engine were killed outright. Several, still alive, shrieked in agony as they futilely attempted to extricate themselves from the wreckage. Here and there a severed arm or leg lay amid the rubble of metal and phosphorus and iron ore.

The last ten cars, however, had been uncoupled by one of the train personnel in time to prevent the entire string of cars from following the engine to disaster.

It was then that the tanks materialized. U.S.-made M-60's, they had once been the property of the Moroccan army, but a year previously they had fallen into the hands of the Polisario. Stark and ominous, they stood out against the lightening horizon as they approached. The chug of their motors and the relentless grinding sound of their treads against the stony surface of the desert could be heard for miles.

Following the tanks, the guerrillas came in a make-shift armada of Jeeps, half-trucks, and self-propelled 155mm guns. Up until this moment, men and equipment had remained in hiding, secure behind the natural ramparts of the low-lying mountains.

Orders to take up position were hastily issued to the Moroccan defenders of the rear cars. Some of the men chose to abandon the train in order to escape or surrender, and as they scrambled out of the cars, they threw down their weapons. But the guerrillas were waiting for them.

Heavy machine-gun and automatic fire tore into them, and they fell into the dust, their blood and torn bodies mingling. In panic, a few tried to turn back, but there was no way they could escape the withering barrage. One soldier made it back to the train, but as he began climbing up a sidecar, a guerrilla turned his Kalashnikov toward him and fired, very casually, sending round after round first into his head, then down the length of his back and into his buttocks. First his skull exploded, then his body seemed to split almost in two. Weirdly he clung to the sidecar for a moment after the firing stopped before tumbling back to the earth.

Now the tanks opened up. Three cars disintegrated in a cloud of brackish smoke and bright yellow balls of flame. Those who survived the holocaust came screaming out of the ruined cars, their bodies blazing, their faces scorched and burned so badly that their skulls showed through. Those who did not immediately collapse were picked off by sharpshooters. At least three men crawled legless from the wreckage; blood trickled from their stumps, some of which continued to burn. They raised their hands in mute appeal for succor, but there was no help to be had.

In a few instances, escaping soldiers fired repeatedly

on their attackers, discharging a series of desperate
salvos. They succeeded in bringing down eight guerrillas
who had carelessly exposed themselves. But there were
well over a hundred men behind them, and they continued to advance, letting out fearsome screams that
seemed to have been borrowed from the jackals inhab-
iting the wilderness.

As the automatic fire of their brothers raged about
them, the guerrillas knocked out the windows of the few
relatively intact cars, shattering the glass with the butts
of their rifles and thrusting their weapons in and firing.

The soldiers who'd started to retreat into the interior
of the cars were shot from behind. Blood showered the
walls and ceilings, and even before the battle ended
desert flies were feasting on the open wounds.

At last the carnage came to a stop and, one by one,
the few soldiers miraculously still alive poured out of
the train, their hands raised high over their heads.
Bound together in a line, the eight men were made to
march single file at gunpoint behind the victorious
troops of the Polisario as they returned to their base.

Two miles from the site of the ambush, several men
were congregated on a rise that offered a spectacular
view of the desert and of the rail line that crept through
it. These were the men who'd orchestrated the attack,
using a two-way radio for communicating instructions
and half a dozen pairs of Nikon binoculars to witness
the operation's success.

The war to secure the independence of the sub-
Saharan territory, once known as Spanish Ifni until the
Spanish gave it up and it became known as Western
Sahara, had been going on for so many years that only
one of the men positioned on the rise had been involved

in the war since the beginning. The objective now was exactly the same as in the mid-1970s—to win independence in the name of the mostly nomadic inhabitants and maintain that independence in the face of Moroccan territorial claims, which continued to be asserted so fiercely because of the valuable treasure of phosphorus lying under the land.

Of those gathered on the promontory, only one was an outsider, an observer sent to monitor the situation in the Western Sahara and to report back to his superiors. His name was Maxim Kolnikov and officially he was a military attaché with the Soviet embassy in Algiers. He was somewhat stout and slow to move, with a protruding belly that was a testament to his love of food and beer. The latter he could obtain only with difficulty in Libya, a country to which he often traveled, for all alcoholic beverages were banned there by the Islamic regime of Colonel Qaddafi. Kolnikov's face and bald scalp were highly colored, almost rubescent, and his features were broad and fleshy, the general impression being such as to earn him the code name "Mr. Clean" within certain intelligence circles in the United States.

He had recently come to this region professing to be an ally of the SADR—the Saharan Arab Democratic Republic, which was the political arm of the Polisario —maintaining that his government and the Algerians were working closely to support the insurgents in their struggle against Morocco. Naturally, he was welcomed at first because his arrival coincided with increased shipments of arms from the U.S.S.R. and Czechoslovakia. The weapons had been coming in daily over the past weeks from both Algeria and the sea, and it was understood by Western intelligence that this stockpiling of arms signaled the start of a new campaign against the government of Morocco.

But now as he stood among these scarred guerrillas bristling with automatics and Nikon binoculars, Kolnikov alone knew what this campaign was to entail and when it was to occur. The date had been carefully planned—even before the recent shakeup in the Politburo—so that any significant movement by the Polisario would complement the actions by the Libyan armed forces against Tunisia. Kolnikov knew that this bloody desert encounter was only a minute part of an elaborate scheme to destabilize the southern tier of the Mediterranean, and that the entire scheme depended on the sort of perfect coordination that was not very likely to succeed. But he knew that such strategic judgments were not his to make. He was only a high-level courier, he thought balefully, a man who slipped back and forth between Algiers and Tripoli and Rabat and Hauza, the last a derelict-looking place on the Seguia River that served as the provisional capital of the SADR. He almost might have been a ghost, except for the immensely important information he carried inside his shining bald head.

Now as the sun rose behind the others, keeping their faces in shadow, the Russian felt a renewal of his discomfort with these guerrillas. Only one of them spoke a language he was familiar with, and this man, called Omar, now stared at Kolnikov with his usual exaggerated suspicion. The long, jagged pink scar and the single sighted eye darting back and forth only increased the feeling of hostility the Russian felt from him.

"You must understand that we fight for ourselves, not for the Algerians, not for the Russians. Only for ourselves," Omar barked.

He jabbed a finger at Kolnikov. But Kolnikov was still trying to make out the other's execrable French.

"Yes, of course, you are fighting for yourselves," he

agreed. "We only wish to assist the cause of peoples' revolutionary movements wherever they may be."

He felt he had to speak in clear-cut terms, even though it made him sound as if he were reciting from *Pravda*. Omar and his friends might exhibit valor and cunning in desert warfare, but they totally lacked political sophistication.

"Otherwise," Omar was warning, "we would have no hesitation in eliminating you as we do the Moroccans."

He made a slashing motion across the base of his throat to emphasize his point.

Kolnikov showed no flicker of reaction, but he decided that next time another courier would have to be dispatched from Moscow to deal with these people; he had had enough.

Another hour had to pass before Kolnikov had sufficiently cooled Omar's hostility and convinced him that the Soviets had the Polisario's best interests at heart. Even so, he wasn't sure he'd altogether succeeded. When the Russian finally left his reluctant hosts, he couldn't escape the fear that one or the other of them might act on his suspicions and put a bullet in his back.

No bullet came. Which was a considerable relief to him, for unlike these men, Kolnikov didn't especially welcome the opportunity to become a martyr. The kind of demise he pictured for himself was always sybaritic and painless—some sort of death among the fleshpots of Paris or New York, a death he trusted would not come his way too soon, for he very much wanted to enjoy those fleshpots before he was obliged to take his leave of them.

7

It was early evening, and in the harsh, sputtering light of the hotel lobby, Maxim Kolnikov looked less like a high-ranking intelligence officer than an overweight businessman hoping to make a deal lucrative enough to put an end to his exhausting odyssey.

In actuality, it had taken him nearly ten hours by two-wheel drive to get from the insurgent encampment to this southern Moroccan city. Bad enough that the motor kept giving out on him, but he had also been compelled to stay off the main highway to avoid border patrols and their questions about what he was doing driving about alone in a war zone.

Relaxing now, he held a drink in one hand while his other rested on a black briefcase on his lap. He was concentrating on the flickering lamp beside him—wondering whether sabotage or routine inefficiency accounted for the phenomenon—when he realized all at once that he was being closely scrutinized by a man standing off to his right.

Kolnikov raised his eyes and saw an unplaceable yet very familiar face. The man had the sort of looks, the Russian saw immediately, that would get him into trouble with women. There was something Levantine about his features, but both the casual way he shifted his weight and the bright, toothpaste smile that he now bestowed on Kolnikov indicated he was an American. Although Kolnikov still couldn't place the features, he knew instinctively that this was no one he wanted to see—especially not here in the south of Morocco.

But the familiar face knew who *he* was, all right.

"So, Maxim, it looks like we've gained a bit of weight. The good life is getting to you, I see."

Now the name came back to him: John Zoccola. They had last met three years previously at the North-South conference in Forte-de-France. Both men had been delegates to the conference, which like its predecessors had failed to accomplish anything approximating a transfer of wealth from the richer countries of the Northern Hemisphere to the impoverished ones of the Southern.

Kolnikov shrugged. Glancing around him at their decrepit surroundings, he said, "The good life. Here?"

Without invitation, Zoccola took the seat beside him.

"What brings you here, Maxim? Just wanted to get away from it all?" he asked gleefully, seemingly vastly amused to have found Kolnikov in this improbable place.

"That's right. I wanted to get away from it all." Kolnikov looked appropriately glum. It wasn't so much that he minded Zoccola spotting him, though he'd have preferred it otherwise. No, what really worried him was the possibility that Zoccola would catch a glimpse of the man he was waiting to meet. Nonetheless, the Russian decided against breaking off the conversation abruptly in the hope that Zoccola would eventually leave of his own accord.

"I understand that your people are shipping some interesting new gadgets to the Polisario," Zoccola said with feigned casualness. "Toys like T-54 tanks and SAM-6 missiles and some FROG-7's and Scud-B SSM's."

"The way you say it," Kolnikov said evenly, smothering his apprehension at the other's probing, "you make them sound like rare zoological finds. To be frank with you, I have no idea what you're talking about. What my government does is of no concern of mine. I am exclusively a merchant of agricultural machinery, hoping to obtain some hard cash for my country."

"Agricultural machinery in the desert?"

"With agronomic advances there is no telling what can be grown out of sand and salt. Look at what the Zionists have achieved, though naturally I wish they'd stuck to farming and left politics to others."

"Well, someday you're going to have to tell me all about these agronomic advances."

"Any time. I will bone up on them, as you Americans say. Now it is your turn. What are you doing in Agadir?"

"Idling away my time. At Club Med."

This was clearly preposterous though there was in fact a Club Med in the vicinity.

"I do hope that you enjoy yourself." Kolnikov no longer had his eyes on Zoccola; he was looking toward the hotel entrance with such intensity that he could almost visualize the man he was waiting for. Unconnected thoughts began to race, panic-stricken, through his mind. The other man was very late. That wasn't unusual in this part of the world. But how could they coordinate the big Polisario strike on the precise day it was scheduled for when one had to depend on such people? But it *was* lucky the man was late today. Perhaps Zoccola would leave soon . . .

Zoccola observed Kolnikov's agitation calmly. "Your problem, Maxim," he said, "isn't that you're necessarily in the wrong line of work, but that you're not being rewarded properly for what you do. What have you got for yourself now? A flat on Arbat Ulitza and a dacha near Zagorsk? It's not bad, Maxim, but, still—two and a half rooms for you and your family?" He shook his head in mock sympathy. "It's nothing like what you could have."

Kolnikov had just moved to the flat on Arbat Ulitza in the center of Moscow, and he was deeply unsettled by the fact that Zoccola was aware of it. Here he'd thought that his movements had gone undetected, certain that U.S. intelligence believed him to be in Helsinki, and now this Zoccola, who was obviously very well-connected, was playing games with him for some apparently specific purpose.

"Am I being shopped?" he asked sharply.

Zoccola feigned shock at the idea. "You know me better than that, Maxim. After all those wonderful conversations we had in Forte-de-France, I'm firmly convinced that you're a loyal Party member and a paragon for millions of impressionable Komsomol youths."

"Is this sarcasm quite necessary?"

"It wasn't my intention to be sarcastic with you, Maxim. In fact, I thought I might find a way to help you out. Should you ever have an urge to settle somewhere other than in Zagorsk, just let me know."

"And how will I do that?"

Before Zoccola could answer, another man, an

American, came into the lobby and joined him. It was Lisker.

Only an hour before, Zoccola had spoken by phone to Lisker, who was now attached to the Moroccan naval command not many miles north of Agadir.

It was Drexell who had linked them up; he alone knew how to reach any member of Triad, and in some respects he was like a puppeteer; his ability to coordinate his subordinates from afar was great, but his motives for doing so were not always apparent, even to those who worked most closely for him.

Enervated by the long hours he'd had to spend with General Haidalla, the pompous Moroccan commander of the region that included the El Jadida monitoring station, Lisker was only too glad to obey Drexell and visit Zoccola in Agadir. Opposite in almost every respect, the quicksilver Zoccola and somber Lisker had begun to develop a curious sort of respect for one another.

In the lobby of the Agadir hotel, he had immediately noticed Zoccola standing beside an overweight, melancholy-looking man. Zoccola had mentioned over the phone that Mr. Clean was expected in Agadir tonight, and Lisker was sure the seated man was he.

Zoccola casually made the introductions.

"Are you also vacationing at Club Med, Mr. Lisker?" Kolnikov asked ironically.

Lisker waited for Zoccola to answer for him. "No, he's here about a boat," the latter replied.

Kolnikov abhorred riddles and remained silent.

"In fact, it's one of your own boats," Zoccola added.

"Boats? What would I, a salesman of agricultural machinery, have to do with boats?" the Russian demanded self-righteously.

"There's a rather large Soviet trawler," Lisker answered in his grave voice. "I suppose you could call it a trawler. It's now trapped by the Moroccans a half-mile offshore, less than an hour's drive from here.''

Kolnikov frowned. He knew the trawler had to be part of the small armada his government had dispatched to supply the Polisario with arms and other war matériel. The loss of whatever was on board this particular trawler would be of little consequence. The problem was that, with the ensuing embarrassment over the discovery of weapons on the trawler, Russia's elaborately orchestrated strategy might begin to unravel.

"Why do you tell me this?" Kolnikov asked, attempting to maintain his innocence.

"I just thought you might be interested," Lisker said slowly. "After all, the boat entered Moroccan territorial waters illegally."

"I don't know anything about this. You see, I've been out of touch and I do not know the most recent news."

What he said was absolutely true, and he silently cursed himself for his ignorance. Since slipping back over the Moroccan border a few hours ago, he'd had no chance to communicate with his Soviet control in Algiers. Nor had he heard anything about this misadventure with the trawler on any of the shortwave foreign language broadcasts. With a melodramatic sigh, he said, "I presume then, gentlemen, that the Moroccan authorities have boarded this trawler."

"Not just yet," Lisker said. "Their naval gunboats have it surrounded, but since the captain of the trawler hasn't been willing to permit anyone on board, the situation's developed into a classic standoff."

Kolnikov's face had become utterly impassive, but his mind was working feverishly. Perhaps there was still time, perhaps somehow through negotiations between

Rabat and Moscow, the trawler could be set free without complications. The worst that might happen, Kolnikov forced himself to hope, was that Moscow might sacrifice the Polisario operation in order to keep the more important Libyan plan going.

At the very moment Kolnikov was thus seeking to reassure himself, into the lobby sauntered the man he had been waiting for well over an hour. Wearing a light jacket and dark slacks, he wouldn't have attracted attention under any other circumstances. But with so few people about, he became particularly conspicuous.

Hemmed in by the Americans, Kolnikov was at first unsure what to do. Even a discreet warning hand signal or movement of the eyes was not likely to go unnoticed.

Abruptly Kolnikov sprang from his chair, gave the two Americans a sickly smile, and announced heartily that he would have to be on his way. Knowing something was up, Lisker turned immediately and caught sight of the man who was scanning the lobby for Kolnikov. As the Russian darted toward the Arab, Lisker pointed out the man to Zoccola, and they both moved to follow the Russian and his friend, who had both just disappeared into the street.

As they moved, Lisker recalled with total clarity the photograph of this same man which he'd been shown at El Jadida three days ago. The man they were following was Ibrahim Brega, the man who had been in charge of the ground station the night the American satellite had performed its disappearing act.

Once outside the hotel, the two Americans looked up and down the block, trying to see by the half-light of the street lamps, but the only person in view was a robed figure slumped in a doorway, a tin can held in his outstretched hand.

A356
   C I CYLCYLUIU - 0970
AM-TUNISIA: EJT, 840

LASERPHOTO VER4

by Lewis Sawyer
Associated Press Writer

TUNIS, TUNISIA, July 24 (AP) — At least thirty
people were killed and over one hundred injured in
an outbreak of violence here last night. Shortly
after eight o'clock, shots were fired in the capital
city of Tunis, when a crowd estimated in the thousands rushed police and units of the armed forces.
The crowd had gathered in the old city in violation
of a curfew imposed the night before by Tunisian
authorities in response to reports about an impending insurrection.

   "It was just chaos," one observer said. "People
were fleeing in every direction, choking from the
tear gas and the smoke bombs police threw into the
crowd."

   The large number of people was apparently in
response to rumors of the possible appearance by
an exiled Islamic fundamentalist leader. The Islamic leader, Salah Adjami, is known for his opposition to the moderate course of the present Tunisian
government. Since 1982, when the government accused him of a role in fomenting disturbances in
various Tunisian cities, the mullah had been living
in permanent exile. According to government
spokesmen, he has been living in Libya as a guest of
Libyan head of state Muammar al-Qaddafi. "He is
Qaddafi's man, all right," noted security adviser
Sayid al-Gazzar, a high-ranking Tunisian official.

8

A further search of the streets around the hotel failed to produce any sign of Brega or Mr. Clean.

Back in front of the hotel, Zoccola told Lisker, "I think he must have taken lessons from Houdini. How could someone that fat vanish into thin air?"

"At least we have some evidence that the Soviets were involved in knocking down our bird," Lisker pointed out. "It's obviously no accident that Kolnikov and Brega were together."

Seeing no reason to persist in a futile search, Zoccola decided to go in and get some sleep. "What about you? You going back to that trawler?"

"That's where Drexell wants me, so that's where I'm going," he said simply.

They shook hands and said good night with some feeling. There was no guarantee they would ever see each other again.

Lisker went to the blue Renault he had parked around the back of the hotel. It had been provided him by the

Moroccan military authorities and worked fine despite some disembodied clanking noises which grew louder as he followed the coast road north toward Cap Rhir. This close to midnight, he had the road nearly to himself, with the Atlantic Ocean a black immensity to his left.

A checkpoint had been set up on P-8 halfway between Agadir and Cap Rhir. Lisker stopped his car, and two groggy officers approached. One immediately recognized him but went through the motions of inspecting his credentials anyway, holding a flashlight up to his papers.

They passed him through, and a short way beyond, just to the side of the road where several military vehicles were parked on the beach, a knot of soldiers stood in the cool breeze from the sea, warming their hands by a small fire.

It was still too far from dawn for Lisker to make out what was happening offshore. All he could discern, silhouetted against the black surface of the Atlantic, was a Moroccan patrol boat, one of two keeping watch over the Soviet trawler. Neither the second Moroccan boat nor the trawler was in view from the beach.

Lisker went over to the waiting motor launch, and one of the sentries spoke to him. "Nothing happens, Mr. Lisker," he said apologetically in French. "All night since you left, always the same. No action."

"We'll have to see what we can do about that," he replied briskly, knowing at the same time that the real action might be transpiring between Rabat and Moscow, not here on the Atlantic coastline.

Lisker and the sentry got into the launch, and in a moment the soldier had started the motor. Twelve minutes later the American was being welcomed on board the Moroccans' Pegasus-class patrol boat by his aide, John Mansfield, who confirmed what the man on the motor launch had said. Since sunset, when Lisker had left for Agadir, the situation hadn't changed at all, and everyone had become resigned to waiting—on this patrol boat and its companion, and apparently on the Soviet trawler too, which was visible from the portside. The only problem was, no one seemed to know exactly what they were waiting for.

This Moroccan Pegasus-class hydrofoil was an advanced craft, over 131 feet in length, and foil-borne as it was, capable of a maximum speed of 48 knots. Perhaps more importantly, it was equipped with eight Harpoon surface-to-surface missiles located aft. In addition, there was a 3-inch 62-caliber gun on the forward end. Altogether it was an expensive and sophisticated vessel, part of a large military aid package to Morocco that the U.S. President had managed to get Congress to pass.

From his position on the patrol boat, Lisker could now see the Russian trawler—its name, *The Karaganda*, was spelled out in bright yellow letters on its bow—sitting stationary approximately 250 yards off the portside. Several Moroccan sailors and their mates were observing the craft with him, passing binoculars from hand to hand. It was the trawler's crew which interested him most, however—the way the Russians seemed to be imitating the Moroccans, peering back at them through binoculars as if they were all involved in some kind of game.

For a trawler, *The Karaganda* was unusually large, both in terms of bulk and length. Lisker estimated that it measured nearly 400 feet from stem to stern. The massive nets that were slung from the decks didn't fool him; he knew the welter of masts and riggings and conning towers hid radar and different kinds of weaponry.

Lisker could still see no good reason why the captain of *The Karaganda* would want to come this close to Moroccan territory. Either some grievous navigational error had occurred or else a storm system sweeping across the Atlantic from the edge of South America had forced the craft off course.

As Lisker watched, a small motorboat was lowered into the water from the trawler's bow. Presently four men clambered down a rope ladder and into the small craft.

"Have you seen Haidalla?" Lisker asked his aide. Mansfield shook his head in disgust.

The man to whom they alluded was the commander of the Moroccan naval contingent guarding the trawler. He was a corpulent, unpleasant man with so many medals and ribbons decorating his uniform that one wondered how he could stand unaided. He also wore an expansive mustache that he took great pains to comb over his lip in a fierce upside-down crescent.

Ever since Drexell had ordered Lisker to return to Morocco from the U.S.S. *Nimitz,* via an Augusta-Bell surface-submarine chopper, he'd constantly been in General Haidalla's company, and it had gotten to be wearing. He had needed the break provided by the side trip to Agadir, but now the break was over.

Lisker called to one of the mates and asked him what had become of Haidalla.

"The General is asleep."

"Go wake him up then."

When Haidalla appeared, he was brandishing a gun, perhaps thinking he might have to take on the Russians singlehanded.

"What is happening here?" he asked Lisker, who was by now inured to the General's demanding manner.

Indicating the small motorboat, now halfway between the trawler and their hydrofoil, Lisker told him they were about to have four visitors.

"But what does this mean?" Haidalla cried out.

"I wish I knew."

The General turned to one of his officers and ordered him to the radio room. "We must inform Rabat," said Haidalla.

Another characteristic of the Moroccan that Lisker had noticed was that, although he had reached the rank of General, he seemed unwilling to make any decisions, no matter how trivial, without authorization from the capital. In a way Lisker couldn't blame him this time. They were dealing with a delicate international situation.

Another five minutes passed before the motorboat came abreast of them. Lines were thrown down so the Russians could secure their boat.

Lisker now saw that one of the four was an officer, most likely the captain. He had a tough, austere face and graying hair; he didn't look very happy.

He was followed by three men whose bluish-gray jumpsuits gave no hint as to their rank.

On gaining the deck, the Russian officers snapped to attention and saluted Haidalla.

Haidalla, seeming uncertain as to the correct protocol, returned the salute a bit warily, as though the gesture represented a compromise.

"I am Captain Oleg Grigenko. These are my men," he announced in English.

The three subordinates gave curt nods.

"I am General Haidalla."

Grigenko didn't seem interested to hear this. "We shall go somewhere and talk?" he said.

Grigenko was one of those natural commanders who couldn't help giving orders, and his words made Haidalla bristle.

Then the General seemed to cave in. "They are talking English," he said apologetically to Lisker and Mansfield. "I do not always understand so good. If you would accompany us—?"

He guided them all belowdecks into the chart room where there were a table and enough chairs to accommodate the group.

A pot of tea was brought in as a display of traditional Moroccan hospitality. The Russians, however, refused it.

Grigenko got right to the point. "How long do you plan to keep us like prisoners here? We are deeply sorry for having strayed into your waters. We were trying to get back into international seas when you interdicted us. We were the victims of a bad storm—our radar was temporarily put out of commission. But you are treating us like pirates. I do not understand."

"You are violating international accords," Grigenko went on, leaving vague which international accords he had in mind. "Our government has made strong representations to your government and I, personally, must warn you of the grave consequences that will follow if you fail to release my boat and let us continue on our way."

Haidalla appeared to be puzzled by the Russian's remarks. "What would you have me do?" he replied helplessly, "This is a matter out of my hands. I can only say to you what we have said many times by radio—that you must allow us to board your vessel. It is very simple. If you are just fishermen, then all will be well."

Grigenko shook his head vigorously. "This is not permitted."

Haidalla replied, "Then I don't know what else we have to discuss," and he stood up with great dignity.

Lisker, who had been sitting across from the Russian the whole time, now spoke. "Captain, where were you headed when you were blown off course?"

"To Accra."

"Not to Dakhla?"

Accra, the capital of Ghana, was far to the south on the western coast of Africa. Dakhla was a port on the coast of the Western Sahara.

"I know nothing of Dakhla," Grigenko said.

At this point of apparent stalemate, Lisker suddenly understood how to deal with the Russians. He could go on guessing forever as to what might have been concealed on the trawler, but he lacked any tangible proof. He saw clearly that the best strategy was now to provoke the Soviets into a foolish reaction, the result of which would be less a military victory for the Moroccan side than a political fiasco for the Soviets.

Lisker got up abruptly and motioned Haidalla to join him on the stairs outside the room.

"What were your last instructions from Rabat?" he asked the Moroccan when they were alone.

"To wait them out. We can possibly starve them."

"I doubt there would be time. I suggest we strike now," he advised.

Haidalla looked alarmed. "What do you mean?" he asked anxiously.

"Keep the captain and his comrades here while we board the trawler. Once we check it out we can let them go."

"But I have no orders!" Haidalla pleaded, unnerved by the American's switch to more aggressive tactics.

"Well, General, what would happen if you were fired on?"

Indignant, Haidalla said, of course he would fire back.

"You wouldn't need to wait for word from Rabat to do so?"

"Of course not. There would be no time."

"Well," he said smoothly, "then no one will accuse you of having done anything provocative."

He could tell that the General was having difficulty following his reasoning. "You are suggesting that the trawler will open fire on us?" Haidalla asked. "It is foolish to think so. What weapons would they use against us?"

"I'll be interested in finding out," Lisker replied innocently, omitting to add that the trawler was probably a disguised supply ship, a modified version of the Ivan Rogov class, and that it was undoubtedly equipped with some very powerful weapons.

"It is too much," Haidalla muttered. "And even if you are right, Mr. Lisker, would the Russians fire on us when we had their captain here with us?"

"I don't know, but it sure would be worth a try," Lisker replied, a slight smile lighting his skeletal features.

Lisker could picture the dilemma of the Soviet crew. Without their captain and their ranking officers aboard, they would probably avoid resisting the Moroccans for as long as possible and instead would start radioing back to Moscow for instructions. Whoever was left in charge of *The Karaganda* would not want to assume responsibility for making the decision to resist.

But Lisker was getting nowhere with Haidalla. He needed to press him further.

"You know that if this succeeds," Lisker told him, "if we get to board *The Karaganda* and find out what they have concealed on it, you're certain to be promoted."

"Yes, that is true," the General said nervously. "But suppose it does not succeed, what then? It is disaster."

"And? Something else is bothering you?"

Haidalla answered stiffly, "It is not honorable to keep the Russian captain and his men as prisoners. It is a breach of hospitality."

"I see. Well then, release them," Lisker told him simply.

"And forget about your scheme?" Haidalla asked.

"I didn't say that. Release them in their launch, *then* strike. At full speed we'll make *The Karaganda* long before they will. By the time they arrive we'll be on board."

Haidalla hesitated. He obviously began to find the scheme credible. Despite the deference to higher authority, his spirit of adventure was finally showing through.

"Yes, yes, this is possible," he agreed tentatively. "I will contact my superiors."

"Then we'll get nowhere," Lisker cut him off. "Your superiors won't be able to make up their minds."

"All right!" Haidalla said, his eyes lighting up. "Then I will have my second-in-command deliver your orders. Meanwhile you must excuse me while I say good-bye to our Russian guests."

Lisker smiled sardonically at the way Haidalla had set up his potential scapegoat; if the enterprise failed, the unwitting subordinate would take the fall. But if it succeeded, Haidalla would step forward to claim that it was he who had initiated the audacious action.

Now events took on a momentum of their own. General Haidalla reentered the wardroom, and Captain

Grigenko, obviously distressed by the implacable attitude of the Moroccan official, quickly strode out, his three mates right behind him. Once on deck, they offered their Moroccan counterparts a series of brusque salutes and climbed back down into their launch, undoing the restraining lines to begin their return journey.

As they departed, orders were going out from the radio room to the second Moroccan patrol boat, positioned to the starboard side of the Russian trawler, alerting its crew to the details of the plan. Both patrol boats would proceed at a speed of 35 knots in the direction of *The Karaganda*, stopping only if the Russians attempted to fire on either craft. In that event further instructions would immediately be issued.

No one was more surprised by the sudden activation of the two Pegasus-class hydrofoils than Captain Grigenko. As the patrol boat he'd just left passed him, nearly swamping his frail motor launch, he stood erect and gazed at it in horror. Although the man operating the launch struggled valiantly to increase its acceleration it was clear that they would never beat the other boats to *The Karaganda*.

As the two patrol boats closed the gap between themselves and the Soviet ship, Lisker could see the empty decks of *The Karaganda* through his binoculars.

"It has a landing platform dock," he advised Haidalla. "Ivan Rogov class."

"And what does that mean?" Haidalla inquired in a bored tone.

"That there could be a whole battalion of marines hidden on board, and maybe as many as forty tanks and some helicopters. It also means that there may be a couple of SAM launchers on it along with a few naval rocket launchers thrown in for good measure."

Haidalla looked suitably impressed, but seemed oblivious to the risks involved in confronting such a vessel.

Should the Soviets decide—independently of Moscow's authorization—to use any of their weapons, there would be no telling what the outcome would be. Lisker was gambling that, like good bureaucrats, they would show restraint, but if they didn't and the Soviets' actions caused an international incident embarrassing to them, this would also redound in favor of the United States.

"There, you can see. They're reacting now," Lisker said, handing the binoculars to Haidalla. In the improving predawn light, Haidalla could see the Russian crew moving frantically back and forth over the decks, the purpose of their movements unclear.

Just as Lisker noticed that three sailors at the forward end of the other patrol boat were preparing to fire, an aide to Haidalla appeared with a report from the radio room. "The Russians are sending a great many signals out," he told the General, "but so far nothing is coming back in."

"A good sign," Lisker observed.

"Give the orders to lower the launches," Haidalla said.

The patrol boat slowed down, and in a few moments three launches, each containing half a dozen men armed with M-16's, were lowered into the water. Twin Browning .30's were mounted at the forward end of each.

Not long after the launches had left the patrol boat, the Soviets finally reacted. What sounded like a Gatling to Lisker began discharging a flurry of rounds which picked up innumerable tiny geysers of water some distance from the launches. A second Gatling—possibly a 23mm—joined in with a chorus of its own.

But the fire failed to reach the three small craft now midway between *The Karaganda* and their patrol boat. As he glanced at the second patrol boat, Lisker assumed that the Soviets were attempting to force the launches to turn back while at the same time avoiding inflicting any injuries on the Moroccans.

It was then that the three twin Browning .30's opened up, and with them the 3-inch .65-caliber gun on the forward end of the patrol boat itself. Whether the fire was being returned spontaneously or on previous orders from General Haidalla, Lisker did not know.

Another two Gatlings on the Soviet craft escalated the engagement; this time the Russian gunners were not nearly so cautious. They turned their weapons directly on the launches.

As the launch closest to *The Karaganda* was peppered with automatic fire, two men were thrown from the craft, blood spurting from the chest wounds. Several others sustained severe injuries and lay thrashing about in the bottom of the launch, their limbs twitching spasmodically as they choked on blood bubbling up from vital organs that had been torn apart.

The lead launch began wobbling dangerously, pitching forward as the fusillade from the Gatlings continued. All at once the entire crew was in the sea, a dozen screaming men struggling to remain afloat in water that was turning the color of blood.

Seeing this, Haidalla drew himself erect and shouted out a magnificent, though completely ineffectual, curse at the Russians.

"I'd suggest you order your men back," Lisker told him, satisfied that they had forced the Soviets to fire first in waters where, legitimately, they had no right to be. This fact would create great embarrassment for Moscow once the world heard about it. And additionally, though they had been denied a look at *The Karaganda* firsthand, at least they now had sufficient evidence to classify the vessel as a covert military supply ship.

But Haidalla wasn't to be stopped now. Where previously he had shown himself too afraid of repercussions from Rabat, by this point he was altogether intoxicated by the passion of combat. Rushing into the command room, he ordered two Harpoon missiles to be launched. Lisker followed him in.

The launch was actuated by a technician's manipulation of a few keys on the computer console in the command room. The console screens held schematic representations of the Russian boat, accurately projected by radar and sonar readings, with the potential target areas on the trawler indicated by a number of small contiguous circles. There were eight circles and eight missiles programmed so that the boat would be struck in its most vital parts. Not all of the missiles would be necessary, of course. As Haidalla had decided, properly directed, the two that had just been launched could debilitate *The Karaganda*, if not demolish it entirely.

As they watched, two contiguous target areas on the screen began blinking; then the blinking abruptly ceased, yielding to a permanent dark green color. A second or two later there were two consecutive concussive roars, so close by that the hydrofoil trembled violently, lurching back and forth with the shock. A spectacular light, fiercely white, filled the open doorway to the command room, making Lisker and the others temporarily blind.

As soon as they regained enough of their sight, Lisker and Haidalla rushed out onto the deck to see what damage the Harpoons had wrought.

Precisely on target, the missiles had struck *The Kara-ganda* amidships, leaving the quarterdeck in shambles, contorting turrets and riggings into a chaotic pile of rubble from which whorls of smoke were now rising. Through gaping holes on the deck, the ruined outlines of several tanks were visible. The trawler itself was pitching wildly after the hit, though it seemed in no danger of capsizing.

Through his binoculars, Lisker could see crewmen running wildly all along the decks, carrying stretchers for the wounded and hoses with which they hoped to extinguish the fires. An alarm shrieked constantly, drowning out the cries of the injured men.

As Haidalla watched the spectacle with obvious satisfaction, the two remaining Moroccan launches started back to the patrol boat. Scattered shots from one of the Soviet's 23mm Gatlings fell harmlessly short of them.

"We shall see what else can be done," declared the Moroccan general, his arms akimbo. He was disturbed that *The Karaganda* was slowly, almost imperceptibly, setting into motion. It was his intention to take it out of action entirely.

Lisker grabbed hold of his arm before he could re-enter the command room. "I don't think another strike would make any sense at this point," he advised the Moroccan sharply.

Haidalla frowned, looking betrayed. "But, you see, it is moving away from here! We must stop it!"

"Do that and you'll find you've overstepped yourself with your bosses. We've accomplished pretty much what we set out to do. We've made the Russians look like fools, and we've established that this is a military supply ship that's evidently part of a massive Polisario buildup."

Haidalla still could not understand why, if that were so, they shouldn't complete what they'd started and knock the Soviet ship out altogether.

Patiently Lisker explained that to do so might lead to a state of war between the Soviet Union and Morocco which, he suggested, Haidalla might not care to be responsible for. "With the engagement broken off at this juncture no one wins and no one loses. The Russians aren't going to continue on to Dakhla. They'll put in for repairs, probably in Malta. And as for any other ships coming, your people will now be prepared for them, and the Russians will have to be more careful."

Haidalla released a protracted sigh. He would have loved to see *The Karaganda* in flames and sinking into the waters.

"I will accept your advice," he said, "but I am not pleased."

The American knew enough to say nothing.

9

Picking up Mr. Clean's trail was a bitch. Zoccola's informants had told him variously that the Russian was still in Agadir, that he had moved on to Casablanca, that he was in Fez, and that he'd left the country and was now in Madrid or Barcelona, but Zoccola was unable to corroborate any of these reports. The most reliable source, a government functionary who'd been in the corridors of power so long that he needed to be taken down from the shelf and dusted off, had said that Mr. Clean was in Rabat. But now that Zoccola was actually in Rabat he wasn't any closer to finding Maxim Kolnikov than he'd been in the south.

Seated in a lounge chair by the side of the pool at the Rabat Hilton, Zoccola stared disconsolately into space, oblivious to everything but the bikini-clad European women swimming back and forth in the chlorine-rich water. As he lay baking in the sun, his low spirits put him in a rare introspective mood.

All his life, he thought, people had called upon him to

mediate, to patch things together when all other avenues had failed. Growing up in the streets of the Bronx, he'd honed his negotiating skills without having any idea they were his ticket out of the slums. His boyhood friends grew up unrestrained. They went in for minor crimes and major drug habits. Skag was a way of life, numbers running a calling like the priesthood. A death by a midnight knifing or a .22-caliber bullet in the gut was a surprise only in its timing, never in the fact that it had occurred. In a physics course at City College in New York, Zoccola had learned that there was such a thing as Heisenberg's Uncertainty Principle. It stated, more or less, that you could never be absolutely certain where anything was at any given time. The principle was applied to atoms and to electrons that danced around the atoms, but Zoccola thought Heisenberg must have come from the Bronx, the home of the uncertainty principle. Death and conflict were everywhere, but, Zoccolo had learned, they could be reined in if you knew how, if you just knew the trick of it.

Zoccola always seemed to know the trick.

He had the knack of coming into the middle of things, turning down a street, for instance, and finding two friends about to bludgeon a third into a coma, and, somehow, skillfully separating the warring parties. "Talk it out," he would say, "let John hear all about it." The only reason he could get away with this, of course, was that he'd managed to acquit himself in enough fights to gain the others' respect. Otherwise he would long ago have been destroyed like so many of the others.

He'd acquired refinement over the years. He learned how to act at receptions in Manhattan penthouses, and he learned how to act in boardrooms with windows opening on vistas of New York harbor.

Much of his success could be put down not just to hard work and native brilliance, but also to the luck of his genes, for he was in fact exceptionally good-looking and had a way of attracting women even when attracting women was the very last thing on his mind. And because these women came from all walks of life, he was provided with access to even more worlds than his talents would otherwise have opened to him.

His many relationships demanded a great deal of juggling, and led to two marriages that had petered out. Technically speaking, Zoccola was still married (though childless); separated now for nearly six years, he and his second wife, Luanne, just hadn't gotten around to the formalities of divorce. They got together from time to time, but only for a couple of hours of amiable conversation, mostly about their current love affairs (never about Zoccola's business and political interests).

With his fate so tied to women, it was little wonder that fate now sent one more across his path.

As she strode past the pool, Zoccola forced himself out of his contemplative mood and gave her his full attention. She was a striking woman, with her dark hair held up and back in an aristocratic style, and she walked with a quick, decisive stride, her long tan legs intermittently revealed by a modest slit in her summery white skirt. Zoccola quickly noticed the two men following her, both with eyes concealed behind polarized lenses. There was no mistaking the pair for anything but bodyguards. Behind their shades, he could just make out their restless eyes surveying the poolside area for any hint of trouble.

The beautiful woman and her bodyguards quickly disappeared into the interior of the Hilton, and Zoccola beckoned a waiter forward to inquire who this woman with the bodyguards might be. The waiter expected Zoccola to order another white wine spritzer (he was drinking it only out of concern for his waistline, not because he actually liked such anemic concoctions). When he asked for the name of the woman, the waiter looked at the poolside walkway that led into the hotel as though trying to rematerialize her image. Then he said, "I think this must be Miss Calenda."

"Calenda? Am I supposed to know who that is?"

"She is the wife of Adam Meureudu, the Indonesian foreign minister."

"She doesn't look Indonesian."

"No, sir. She is American. May I get another drink for you?" the waiter asked, seguing into his usual role.

Zoccola realized that his glass was nearly empty. "Why not?" he shrugged.

Later that evening in the Hilton nightclub, he was still consuming white wine spritzers, but at a more considered rate. Impatient and restless as he waited for new orders from Drexell, he had earlier resigned himself to exploring the full range of facilities the hotel had to offer. Despite the hotel nightclub's good reputation, however, all he'd seen were the predictable belly dancers.

Shortly before eleven a middle-aged man in an impeccably tailored white suit entered the club, accompanied by an entourage of Europeans, as well as a pair of unsavory-looking bodyguards. On the shortish side and with pitch-black hair, the man had the eyes of a predator.

As they took their seats at one of the large corner tables, Zoccola saw that the woman from the pool was in the group. No longer in white, she now wore a shimmering dress that shone with the colors of the Mediterranean, sometimes blue, sometimes green, depending on the amount of light cast on it. And it was, he noted admiringly, cut sufficiently low to keep his eyes riveted on her.

He guessed that the short man with the hungry eyes must be her husband, Adam Meureudu, the Indonesian foreign minister.

With his attention so distracted, Zoccola didn't realize until they'd started that the belly dancer had been replaced by a native band armed with guitars, snare drums, and other indigenous instruments. With extreme enthusiasm they played a string of strange-sounding versions of British and American rock songs.

Zoccola was wondering how much more of this entertainment he could take when a young man he had never seen before approached his table. "There is someone who wishes to speak with you," the stranger said softly.

"And who is this someone?" Zoccola asked, intrigued.

The messenger shrugged. "I do not know. A man asks me to tell you this, that is all."

"What does this man look like?"

Another shrug. "He looks like a man."

"Did he mention what he wants to speak to me about?" Zoccola asked impatiently.

"He says that it is important."

"Fine. And where is this man of yours?"

"I will take you to him."

"You're sure you're not making a mistake . . ."

"You are Mr. John Zoccola?"

"You got him."

One or two fewer white wine spritzers and he might have chosen not to pursue the odd summons. But he was restless and just curious enough to follow this through.

As he left the nightclub he circled around the Calenda woman's table and overheard her being addressed as

Adrienne. Well, now he had her full name, he thought with satisfaction.

At the exit he turned for a last look at her. She had her back to him, but he enjoyed the sight of her long black hair lying along the slope of her bare shoulders.

Once outside in the lobby, Zoccola saw that the young man who'd led him from the nightclub now appeared to have vanished. As he cast his eyes about the lobby, two men moved swiftly up to him. Both were wearing sports coats and appeared to be businessmen, but unlike most businessmen, they carried guns, a fact they conveyed to Zoccola by discreetly thrusting their barrels against his rib cage.

"We regret having to do this, Mr. Zoccola," said the stouter of the two, "but we are under instructions to have you come with us. Please try and avoid creating a disturbance."

With the press of the two guns against his chest, Zoccola had no intention of creating a disturbance. "Can I ask where we're going?"

"There is someone who wishes to speak to you; that is all I can say."

"Maybe next time he could try the telephone," Zoccola said sharply.

His two companions didn't share his sense of humor. They solemnly escorted him out of the lobby over to a white Mercedes. As they motioned him in, Zoccola asked if they'd be traveling very far. There was no response, and he obediently climbed into the back seat of the Mercedes.

10

The phone rang in William Drexell's apartment on Vermont Avenue at 2:15 in the morning. It was Morse Peckum, asking if Drexell could be at the Situation Room in half an hour.

"I'll give it a try," Drexell responded groggily. "What's it about?"

"I can't say now."

Drexell grunted and hung up. Despite his best efforts, he was late and the last person to arrive. The President and Peckum were there and so too were Schelling and Secretary of Defense Martin Rhiel, who had brought some charts and maps with him. It was all rather more impressive than the last meeting with the President.

"Come in, William," the President said when Drexell appeared in the door to the room. "Sorry about getting you out of bed."

"I'm used to it," Drexell replied goodnaturedly.

He took a seat and pulled a cigar from his inside coat pocket, eliciting a dirty look from Schelling, who abhorred the smell of smoke.

"From all the reports we're receiving," the President

began, "there's no question that the situation in the North African region has deteriorated dramatically in the forty-eight hours since we last met. As far as the Kremlin goes, we still don't know precisely who is in charge. Kadiyev appears to be in control, but we have nothing firm on that."

"Excuse me, Mr. President," Schelling said. "The Soviet watch desk told me just before I came over here that we can expect—and this is a quote—'an announcement of major importance' some time tomorrow morning, Eastern Daylight Time, from the Politburo. This was from a Polish language broadcast of Radio Moscow. So far there's been no other confirmation."

"All right then. Now maybe they'll finally straighten out the mess their leadership's gotten into. What's the latest on the Black Sea Fleet?" he asked Rhiel, who sprang to his feet.

"Our latest projections," the Defense Secretary explained, "show that the Soviets currently have as many as sixty large surface vessels in the Mediterranean and at least fifteen submarines. We still don't have the precise figures for all the bombers and support craft, but we do know that many of the larger surface vessels are Kirov-class heavy cruisers. They are equipped with vertical takeoff Yak-36 aircraft, replacing helicopters of the Kiev and Minsk type."

The President, Drexell noted, was frowning.

"Of course the Soviets have problems. The only bases for their fleet are in Syria, Malta, and in Libya."

"According to your data is that where the Black Sea Fleet is headed—toward Libya?"

"It certainly looks that way, sir. The lead craft are already reported in the Gulf of Sidra. That doesn't rule out the possibility that a portion of the fleet won't separate and continue into Tunisian or Algerian waters."

"Or Moroccan waters," Drexell added.

"Do you have any reports of supply ships steaming south?" the President asked.

"Quite a few," Drexell said in his rough, commanding voice. "There are an unusually large number of trawlers and freighters in the Atlantic waters off Morocco, most of them of Soviet origin. There are also a large number of vessels in the area that are registered to a charter company in London that's known to contract with the Soviets, supposedly to ship oil. We suspect strongly that the supplies are heading for the Western Sahara where the Polisario are expected to begin a major action against the Moroccans shortly."

Drexell stopped his summation without describing the encounter between the Russian trawler and the Moroccan gunboats. He had fully briefed the President on the engagement earlier, and was not about to create jealousy by suggesting he had sources that Schelling and Rhiel were not privy to. Nor, without positive information on it yet, was Drexell about to touch on the recent satellite downing.

"What's the status of the Sixth Fleet?" the President demanded, turning to the Secretary of Defense.

Rhiel explained that it was almost up to full strength, with two nuclear aircraft carriers, the *Nimitz* and *Enterprise*, and two conventional carriers, the *Forrestal* and the *Midway*. The *Kennedy* was undergoing repairs at the naval base in Rota, Spain. Of the fifteen surface ships available, ten were accompanying the *Nimitz* on a southwesterly course that would take them into Tunisian waters within twenty hours. Five others attached to the fleet were at their home ports in Gaeta, Naples, and Rota. Also, with the fleet were four nuclear-powered submarines; two others were at the special docks at La Maddalena, Sardinia.

"How soon can you get our ships out of port and with the main fleet?"

"Possibly forty-eight hours, sir."

"Then do it." The President turned to Drexell again. "How do you see this—" he was hunting for the right word, "—this mess?"

"It seems to me that the Soviets are trying to orchestrate things in North Africa, and on a grand scale. They seem to be preparing to back up Qaddafi in whatever aggression he's up to, and to give a push to the Polisario in the bargain. There've been rumors for some time that there are up to a hundred fifty Soviet advisers in Tripoli and Tobruk to make sure the Libyans can handle the advanced weaponry the Russians are cramming down their throats. I wouldn't be surprised to see a few Cubans, Czechs, and East Germans around there as well."

"What degree of defense readiness do you think we'd have to go to for the Russians to take notice?"

"I'd say we'd have to go to DefCon III, Mr. President," Drexell said. "Anything less and they're just not going to see it." Normally U.S. armed forces, including the Strategic Air Command, were at Defensive Condition (DefCon) IV or V.

"Do you agree?" the President asked Rhiel.

"I would tend to, yes," he replied carefully.

"Then let's do it, beginning at, say, noon, Eastern Daylight, tomorrow. Is there any problem with that?"

"No problem, sir," said Rhiel.

For a moment the President looked rather pleased with himself. At least, he thought, the Soviets would see that the United States was reacting.

"Could you explain something to me," he said to Drexell after a short pause. "Why don't these people running Tunisia take some sort of action about this Libyan thing? We keep passing them the intelligence we have regarding Libyan military movements, they thank us, and then do nothing. I just don't understand."

"It's the same old story, sir—lack of trust. They believe that we're using the Libyan threat as a ruse to throw the Bourguibas out of office and install somebody we like better. They say that they know Qaddafi and aren't afraid of him. Instead they figure their real problem lies with the Islamic fundamentalists, who cause the kind of disturbances that happened a few days back."

"It can drive you crazy trying to save a country when the people who live there don't seem to want to be saved."

Drexell nodded sympathetically.

The President suggested they move to the problem of speaking to the Soviet Ambassador, Ilya Rudnitsky. The notion of disrupting his sleep seemed to amuse him. "Jeffrey," he said to the Secretary of State, "I want you to have a talk with him, see if you can't deduce what it is his country's up to in the Mediterranean. Turn all the screws you can on the son of a bitch. Make him squirm. It'll do him good."

More than two hours later, a two-tone Lincoln limousine pulled up to the rear of the State Department building. With a security guard by his side, Ambassador Rudnitsky hurried inside.

Unlike his predecessor, Rudnitsky was a very formal man, an Old World European with a taste for classical music and aged French cognac. Even in the middle of the summer, he was never known to appear in public without a suit and tie, a style of dress which seemed to put others in an inferior position. His face suggested more than formality, however. Lean and angular, his features would have suited Cassius, the assassin of Caesar. It was a face that had never known a childhood.

He was ushered into Schelling's office and even at this

dim hour of the early morning, bore himself like an aging aristocrat.

Schelling and the Russian shook hands stiffly. There was an interpreter present in the room, but as Rudnitsky's command of English was exceptional, he was never needed. Schelling only had the interpreter present in the event that Rudnitsky should suddenly pretend that he had lost his command of the English language.

"I apologize for having you come at this awkward time," Schelling said, "but the President agreed that the situation warranted it."

Rudnitsky regarded him quizzically. "Which situation, Mr. Secretary, are you referring to?"

"I am referring to the buildup of your naval and air forces in the western Mediterranean. We have information that leads us to believe that the Black Sea Fleet is about to deploy itself in Libyan waters."

"Since you possess highly advanced reconnaissance satellites and aircraft," Rudnitsky countered in a perfectly even, calm voice, "I would expect that you have better knowledge of this matter than I do. What puzzles me is why you have woken me up to speak to me about this. Just as you maintain your Sixth Fleet in the Mediterranean so we do the same with our fleet. That the number of ships and planes may differ from one day to the next goes without saying. I do not see the reason for your present concern. As you know, we do have the right to use the port of Tripoli. There is nothing so unusual about that."

"We believe," Schelling warned, "that the movement of your fleet is connected to certain military operations currently under way in the Western Sahara and on the Libyan-Tunisian border. The President has instructed me to tell your government that any provocation by either Libyan forces against Tunisian sovereignty or by Polisario insurgents against Moroccan sovereignty will be regarded as aggression by the Soviet Union itself.''

"Forgive me if I do not take you seriously, Mr. Secretary,'' the Russian said the instant Schelling had stopped speaking. "But your allegations are fanciful. What the Libyans do and what the Polisario do is beyond our control. You are in the habit of blaming us for all the troubles that spring up everywhere in the world, but to engage in such fabrications will only heighten international tensions and accomplish nothing. I strongly urge you to advise your President that while the Soviet Union always stands in support of liberation movements we will do nothing to bring the world to the brink of war. On the other hand, the Soviet Union will not sit by and allow imperialist forces to intervene to crush those movements. That has traditionally been our policy and nothing about it has changed since we last met.''

Schelling could see that nothing was going to come of this exchange. But perhaps he could extract from Rudnitsky a useful disclosure in another area. "Off the record, Ilya, could you tell me if Kadiyev has in fact been named First Party Secretary?''

"That is correct. This has been announced already in previous Tass dispatches.''

"But he has made no statement, he has not been seen, and we do not know who to deal with in Moscow.''

"I will convey any message you might wish to transmit,'' Rudnitsky said firmly. "And I must remind you that this obsession with personality that you Americans have is absolutely irrelevant insofar as we are concerned. Since we have a collective leadership, worrying over whether this man or that man is First Secretary merely clouds the issue.''

"And what, Mr. Ambassador, *is* the issue?''

Looking back at him, Rudnitsky maintained a perfect silence.

11

After being in Tunis for four days, Jerry Hahn had left by bus for the south. He was one of the very few foreigners who dared to use such an unprotected means of transportation, but he had a perfectly plausible cover—that of an anthropologist on a foundation grant who was trying to stretch every penny. And from the way he dressed, in starched whites and with eyes glinting myopically from behind thick bifocals, no observer would have any reason to suspect otherwise.

"Aren't you afraid of all the trouble?" asked the man beside him on the bus, a schoolteacher returning to his home in Sousse.

"Trouble?" Hahn looked appropriately perplexed. "Oh, yes. Of course you mean the radicals."

Hahn knew very well what the schoolteacher was alluding to. In the four days he had been in the capital he'd witnessed a succession of disturbances created by the adherents of Salah Adjami, mullah and leader of a fanatical sect of Islamic fundamentalists. They had repeatedly taken to the streets and rioted within the walls of the medina, and it was all the security forces could do to prevent the outbreak from spreading into the new city. Martial law had been proclaimed and soldiers, with tanks to back them up, had taken up position at strategic intervals along major streets and boulevards.

For the most part Hahn had remained sequestered in his hotel room, listening to the rattle of gunfire and the occasional detonation of an explosive charge. Once a blast occurred so close by that the walls of his room shuddered and bits of plaster rained down, covering his hair and shoulders with a layer of white.

It had been frustrating being confined to his room, but there was no helping it. With the city in such turmoil, with dusk-to-dawn curfews in effect, movement had been severely limited. Hourly there were rumors of coups, riots, revolutions, and outright war. Government assurances that the situation was under control only met with derision on the part of the populace. Hahn didn't have to go far to divine the people's feelings. The porters and waiters he encountered at his hotel were constantly speculating as to when the government would collapse.

The only times he got outside he was obliged to make his travels in Moroccan government limousines. Any American or European spotted in certain parts of the city was liable to be set upon by angry crowds and, indeed, by the time he left Tunis, at least five Westerners had been killed and another forty hospitalized in such attacks.

From the ministers and security officials he spoke to, Hahn had been able to learn practically nothing that he didn't already know from radio and newspaper reports. His main source of information was derived from operatives in Triad's employ, native Tunisians who could wander about the old city at will and bring back word for him at the hotel as to what was really happening in the capital. Their reports were, of course, very much at variance with those of the government, which was trying to put the best light on an extremely delicate situation.

It was these operatives who told him just how influential the fundamentalist Moslems were in the country. There were far more extremists than he'd ever imagined. The fact that Tunisia was among the most progressive and pro-Western states in the region disguised the fact that it was also fertile breeding ground for violent religious fervor.

But the Mullah Salah Adjami, who'd come out of the desert many years before railing against pernicious and satanic Western influence and his country's corrupt leadership, had touched a responsive chord. The students especially had been attracted to his militant brand of Islam, which took its cue from the Mullah's Iranian counterpart, the Ayatollah Khomeini.

Hahn suspected, because of the Mullah's timing, that he was a Libyan plant. This was not to say that he wasn't sincere in his zealotry, but, wittingly or not, he was being used to advance Libyan—and by extension, Soviet—interests in the region. A revolution in the name of Islam which succeeded in toppling the pro-Western regime of Tunisia would promote Qaddafi's objectives every bit as much as armed intervention.

The previous day, Hahn had finally contacted Drexell on a secure line out from his hotel. Drexell, after hearing all his operative had learned, ordered Hahn to the south, closer to the Libyan-Tunisian border. "The latest information we've gotten," he'd told Hahn, "is that the Mullah is somewhere in the direction of Libya, in the area of Medenine. I want you to see if you can find out exactly where he is.''

''And then?''

''And then we'll talk again.''

Hahn was dubious about the prospect of finding the Mullah, but he was even more dubious about Drexell's decision to send him in the direction of the Libyan border. Since his arrival in the country, rumors, never fully confirmed, had been circulating warning of an impending war. Drexell's agents in Tunis informed Hahn that armored Tunisian units and infantry were gathering on the frontier in preparation for just such a war. Drexell himself told Hahn that aerial reconnaissance photos showed a massing of Libyans on their side of the border, but it still wasn't clear whether these were armed units or simply thousands of peasants.

One thing was clear, though—Hahn was heading into a part of the country where the government exercised little, or no, authority and where if he should find himself in peril, there'd be absolutely no one to come to his aid.

Before ending their conversation, Drexell had explained how Hahn was to get in touch with a man, an asset of Triad's, in Medenine. But whether the man could actually be found was another matter entirely. If Tunis was in chaos, why should Medenine, which was so close to Libya, be any safer?

After the long, bumpy, dusty ride on the bus from Tunis, Hahn got off at a desolate little town whose only commercial establishments were a small café and a gas station. Just as Drexell had predicted, a Renault was waiting for him, courtesy of one of their contacts. The keys were in the glove compartment, also as he'd been told.

As he drove, Hahn was glad that the highway south to

Medenine was devoid of any traffic except for Tunisian military vehicles. The vast majority of them were heading in the opposite direction—north—away from where the fighting was expected to occur. He seemed to be the only one going toward the trouble.

Why am I doing this? he kept asking himself as the suicidal nature of his mission became clearer and clearer.

He wondered whether he should have protested when Drexell ordered him to Medenine. It was true that he was the one member of the team best equipped to assess what was about to happen in the area. He'd traveled extensively through the Maghreb in years past, was fluent in Arabic, and possessed an impressive knowledge of Arab culture and politics. But how was such knowledge and linguistic ability going to help him survive?

On the other hand, when Drexell had said that he needed him to be his eyes, Hahn had felt the full warmth of Drexell's trust. He could not betray such trust.

Despite the fear, Hahn also couldn't deny the rare sense of excitement, the charge of adrenaline that shot through him.

But he kept returning to the same questions: Could he pull this off? And, could he pull this off and come out of it alive?

Toward nightfall, he spotted a ghostlike form rising from the desert about five miles ahead. As he approached, he saw it was a tank and that it was traveling away from him in a line approximately parallel to the road.

He brought his car to a halt. Soon a second tank came into view, then a third, and he began to detect the sound of their engines and the noises of sand and pebbles sputtering beneath their treads. When a fourth tank materialized, Hahn realized they were in formation and seemed to be heading toward Medenine.

With his field glasses, he made out their markings. Libyan, he saw with a jolt. But he didn't know why he should have been surprised.

For some reason he thought of how Judith, his estranged wife, always accused him of being on the periphery of things, of watching from the sidelines while life went on without him. What, he wondered, would she think of him now?

It was obvious the tanks hadn't taken notice of him, thanks to his having killed his headlights the instant the first tank had come into view.

Nonetheless, he wasn't prepared to risk continuing along the main highway; there was no telling how many more tanks he'd encounter if he did.

He turned off the road onto the desert and began a long bumpy ride south. As the evening grew darker, he thought he'd lost sight of the road, and this worried him more than the Libyan tanks. If, come morning, he found himself in the desert with only a depleted thermos of water, he would soon die of thirst, a fate he judged worse than a quick death by a Russian bullet.

Though he now knew for certain that a Libyan military action was under way, he hesitated about alerting Triad until he could better assess its exact nature—was it a strategic probe, a provocative move, or a full-scale invasion?

By the time the first rays of the sun reached him the next morning, the desert floor was eerily still. Hahn could no longer detect the sound of tanks or of anything other than the call of great-winged black birds that swept through the sky in search of prey. He was grateful, however, to discern the dark asphalt ribbon of highway in the distance. He hadn't strayed far off it after all.

When Hahn tried his AM radio he succeeded in obtaining a barrage of martial music, then a lilting romantic ballad by an Algerian vocalist, and finally the shrill, accusatory voice of Salah Adjami himself, exhorting the masses to revolt and oust their oppressors.

"Death to the Americans, death to the Westerners!" he repeated over and over again.

As he continued driving on the desert parallel to the highway, Hahn listened for the better part of an hour, curious to see how this radical station would announce its identity.

At last the Mullah fell silent and an announcer said, "You are listening to the Voice of Free Tunisia. We will return to the air at twelve noon. Please be with us then."

Hahn guessed that the lulls in the transmission were so the transmitter could be moved from one location to another to escape detection.

Meanwhile, since the road had been free of vehicles since sunup, he felt reassured enough to rejoin it.

After driving for half an hour, he came upon a column of peasants that extended for almost a mile along the shoulder of the highway. Practically all of them— men, women, and children alike—were dressed in robes, and many of them hefted baskets and bulging suitcases that looked as though they might split apart and release their contents at any moment. There were a few antiquated trucks accompanying the column, their open carriages crammed full of people.

When he passed them, the people scarcely looked up at him. They had doubtless seen vehicles of far greater interest in the course of their trek.

As he sped past, Hahn felt sure this must be part of the migratory wave that the reconnaissance pilot had observed several days previously.

He speculated that it would not be enough for Qaddafi to stage an armed invasion of Tunisia. His end was an actual merger of states, an Islamic republic which embraced both Libya and Tunisia. This would give him credibility as well as power, and the world could not then so easily dismiss him as a sword-flailing madman. These peasants were the front line of the assault. Using them, Qaddafi could say that the people had taken it upon themselves to unite their two countries.

Moreover, given the length of the frontier and the terrain through which it ran, there were even fewer means of halting a migration of unarmed peasants than of halting tanks and infantry.

It finally struck Hahn that the peasants, with their trucks and camels and donkeys, provided both a cover and camouflage for the Libyan army as it assembled on the other side of the border.

A few miles later the road descended and Hahn realized that he had entered Medenine. Everywhere he looked people were running for safety through the narrow, twisted streets. Small children dazedly took refuge in doorways to avoid being trampled underfoot, and dogs howled balefully in dissonant counterpoint to the ululating voice of the muezzin who was at the moment reciting the morning prayers through a loudspeaker. Adding to the din were the horns of cars and buses and broken-down trucks, all seeking means of escape. While the Libyans hadn't actually gotten here yet, it was obvious they were expected at any minute.

How Hahn was to find his asset was beyond him. His contact in Tunis had given him the address, but in this confusion, Hahn wasn't sure he'd be able to get through.

He drove his Renault as far as he could, then parked it on a dead-end street.

After getting out and locking his car, he stood to observe the scene about him for a while. By now a cloud of dust, stirred up by the crowds of fleeing people, had risen over the town, casting a yellowish veil over the rich blue sky. The blare of horns was unrelenting, and every so often what sounded like a gunshot, but was more probably a truck backfiring, punctuated the cacophony.

Much to his surprise, Hahn found himself neither very tired—though he knew he should be exhausted—nor very anxious. To the contrary, he felt almost calm and blessed with a confidence that was at obvious variance with his circumstances.

He set out toward what seemed to be the center of the town. In their desperation to escape, people pressed him on all sides as they did their utmost to keep their belongings above their heads. Everyone was shouting, though to whom wasn't clear.

As Hahn worked his way down a narrow street that descended a hill, it was difficult going, not only because of the crowds but also because there was a great deal of gutter water spilling out into his path. The way was both slippery and foul, and Hahn hurried on to get past it to where he could breathe again.

Hahn expected to have seen at least some policemen by now, but he hadn't seen a single one since leaving his car. It was possible that the police had fled in advance of the general population.

At last he came to a nearly empty marketplace of shuttered stalls, and for an instant Hahn had the sense that despite the nearby chaos, he was nearly alone in the world. As he took a few steps across the cobbled surface of the square, however, there was a clap like thunder, and another, and another, and he realized these were the sounds of a battle a long way off. After these rumbling sounds of an artillery exchange, a jet fighter screamed overhead, sweeping eastward so fast that it was impossible for him to determine its make or allegiance. At least if it was foe, Hahn thought gratefully, it hadn't dropped any bombs on them.

To the north of Medenine, Hahn could just make out a squadron of helicopter gunships coming into view. Shrouded behind the cloud of dust hovering above the town, they looked especially ominous: gray, tubular shapes with their artillery protruding like rigid sexual organs. Again Hahn couldn't discern their markings but took some comfort in the fact that they were heading toward the Libyan border and not away from it. He assumed that these were American-supplied Tunisian gunships, probably just shipped in over the last few days.

Leaning against a blank stucco wall of the marketplace, Hahn realized he had thoroughly lost his bearings.

Before too long a young man with a vaguely academic air wandered up to him. Unlike everyone else Hahn had seen, he displayed no sense of urgency whatsoever.

"You speak English?" he asked.

Hahn said that he did and asked him if he knew where he could find a certain Jamal Azhmeh.

"The tanner?"

"Yes, that would be him."

"If he is still here he will be in the *souk*, down in that direction." The young man gestured toward a labyrinthine quarter of town.

Hahn thanked him and went off to explore the nearly empty *souk* without the faintest hope that he would find Jamal Azhmeh, tanner by trade and U.S. intelligence asset by inclination. After all, Drexell admitted earlier that they had been unable to raise him by radio for days, and there was little reason to expect to come across him in person now, certainly not in the middle of an invasion.

And yet, against all odds, Hahn did manage to discover him. Jamal Azhmeh might be the most imperiled citizen in all of Medenine should the Libyans arrive and begin a hunt for American agents, yet here he was, in the same place he was every day—in the rear of his dimly lit shop, where the smell of raw and treated leather was powerful enough to knock a stranger on his ass.

A wiry man with a thin mustache drooping down over his lips, his brow was knitted permanently into an expression of disgruntlement. When Hahn entered his shop, he spat noisily, plugged another wad of Persian tabac into his pipe and lit it.

"You have come to see me about the Mullah," he said, taking the initiative.

"You are Jamal Azhmeh?" Hahn said, backtracking.

"I am who you are looking for. I was told someone would be coming. I think that is you, no? Come, we do our business here."

He rose and motioned Hahn behind a red velvet drape he'd strung over the doorway to a back room.

The back room was smaller than the shop proper; there was a square green table in it and some rickety chairs, one of which he pulled out for Hahn.

In this place the convulsions of distant mortar barrages were muted. What you mostly heard of the outside world were dogs barking as if they'd all gone mad, as well as screaming children, aroused by the excitement of the moment.

"What do you wish to know about the Mullah?" Azhmeh asked agreeably.

"Where he is, for one thing."

"Not far from here. This place or maybe some place

else will become his headquarters. He and the soldiers of the Al-Jihad will soon set up a permanent radio station and begin broadcasting to Tunisia, telling all the people to rise up. He is a very passionate speaker; you must listen to him sometime."

"He is. I know that. But I've been troubled by the question of why he would reveal himself to the people when he is profiting so much from rumors that he is now in prison."

"When he reveals himself," answered Azhmeh as if answering a riddle, "everything will have changed."

"Your sources are reliable?"

"They are very good."

"When is the Mullah expected to come here?"

"Here or another place," cautioned Azhmeh, "but close by. As to when . . ." He responded with a dramatic shrug of his shoulders. "The Mullah is a mysterious man. He comes and goes like a ghost. But his army will soon come to Medenine."

"The soldiers of Al-Jihad?"

"That is correct. They come in the trail of the Libyans."

"When you say soon, what do you mean?"

Here Azhmeh pulled open a secret drawer beneath the table. Inside it were a PK Walther, a Beretta of uncertain vintage, and the sort of snub-nosed .22 favored by New York muggers.

"I mean very soon. And I will be ready."

It struck Hahn that Azhmeh was either a very courageous or very foolish man. "There will be many of them and only one of you," he warned.

"No, this is not true. There are two of us—me and you."

Hahn didn't think that that made the odds any more

reasonable. He asked Azhmeh if he had a telephone or knew where he could locate one.

"Yes, I have a telephone. But it will be of no use to you. Since early last night the lines have been down."

"You have a radio then?"

"A radio to talk to Tunis?"

"That's right, Tunis or elsewhere."

"I have such a radio. But it is not the best. It comes and it goes."

"Well, shall we see how it's performing now?"

Despite Hahn's attempts to appear in control, he suddenly felt exhausted and was grateful when a young boy appeared, bearing a tray with a cup of strong Turkish coffee. It tasted like mud, but went quite a way toward restoring him.

The tanner opened a closet in back of them and with an audible groan lifted a bulky old shortwave radio over to the table, which sagged under its weight.

Hahn regarded the great silver hulk with admiration. The radio must date back to the 1950s, he thought. No wonder, in the words of Azhmeh, it came and went. It was a miracle that it functioned at all.

Azhmeh played with the knobs for the better part of an hour, producing by turns emissions of static, Morse code, and occasionally a garbled voice. When he was satisfied that he'd tuned it as well as it was ever going to be, he concentrated his attention on the transmission system.

Azhmeh knew which wavelength to transmit on, but Hahn wasn't optimistic.

Azhmeh gave his code name, then launched into a frenetic stream of Arabic. In a moment he stopped, stared at the microphone in his hand, then switched to receive. He waited. And waited.

Perhaps no one was out there, Hahn thought. But if there was, he knew he was reduced to depending on this one obstinate tanner to make contact with him.

Again Azhmeh tried, fine-tuning his instrument even further. This time he was rewarded with a crackling burst of sound. It was hard for Hahn to tell what significance the noise had, if any.

"We shall do this again, yes?" the Arab said in his friendly manner, and Hahn agreed enthusiastically.

The same process was repeated once more. Now the signal was much clearer. Hahn could make out the sound of a human voice. Someone was out there after all!

Communication established, the tanner turned the radio over to Hahn, who told the contact to patch them into Clausewitz. He emphasized that De Stael urgently needed to speak with him, and rattled off a series of coded numbers that indicated an emergency condition.

As Hahn waited for the connection to be achieved, Azhmeh sat rocking gently in his rickety chair, completely ignoring his guest.

Twenty minutes passed with infinite slowness before the radio crackled again. "This is Tunis," they heard in an English heavily weighted with an Arabic accent. "We have Clausewitz."

At that moment they seemed like the most beautiful words anyone had ever said to Hahn.

"De Stael here," Hahn called enthusiastically into the mouthpiece. "I read you."

Drexell sounded as though he were on Mars or underwater, his voice thin and remote. "Have you reached our asset?" he asked.

"He's right here."

"What's your situation?"

"Unclear, and unenviable."

"In two days time, at coordinates east forty-two, west sixty-six, at twenty-two thirty hours we'll have some people show up to help you. Their names are Hunt and Shaw. If this presents a problem, contact me later and we'll set something else up."

Hahn memorized the coordinates against the time when he could finally consult his maps. He assumed that the rendezvous point would be close to Medenine.

"Tell me, what's happening there?" Drexell asked, and Hahn explained as best he could about the invasion in progress, but said that he was still unsure as to how big an operation it was or what the military objectives might be. It could be limited to the border area, or it might only be a prelude to an attempted takeover of the entire country.

"And what about Gropius?"

Gropius was the code name given to the Mullah.

"He's due here soon. No one knows when, but I'd say as soon as the adversary has this place secured."

"What do you think about having Gropius neutralized?"

Hahn didn't like the sound of this. "What do you mean by that, sir?"

"Cancelling his contract. Either holding him incommunicado—"

"Kidnap him?"

"—or eliminate him from the picture entirely."

Hahn thought that either action would run the risk of backfiring. "If something like that happened," he pointed out, "we'd be blamed whether we were responsible or not. It would only incite the populace further."

There was such a long silence on the other end that Hahn feared the communication had been broken. But then Drexell finally resumed speaking. "I had a feeling you'd say that. Well, see if you can't stay on top of him when he does arrive. In the meantime I'm working on something that should give the Libyans second thoughts about launching an invasion.''

"You have another operation in mind?"

"Don't worry, you won't miss out on it."

"That's what worries me," Hahn laughed.

Drexell laughed too, although Hahn hadn't been entirely joking. It was no joke that he was scared. But Drexell wasn't interested in that side of things. The boss either didn't know what fear was like or else he'd forgotten long ago.

12

Zoccola came awake with a start, and for the first few moments of consciousness he had absolutely no idea where he might be. How long had he been asleep? he wondered, looking at the yellow-painted stucco ceiling. He didn't know that either. Glancing at his watch, he saw that it was a little past eight, and by the sunlight pouring in through the arched window over his bed he saw that it was morning.

The room was comfortable enough, brightly painted and filled with the scent of hibiscus and jasmine. When he got up off the bed and looked out the window he saw an unusual sight: a crumbling fortification with a succession of ramparts and towers. To have reached its current state of decomposition, it must have been deteriorating for hundreds of years. To the right of this structure Zoccola could see a mosque that was also in a state of decay. Everywhere, though, there were flowers and shrubbery, and from time to time he observed a stork descending from the sky, disappearing in the direction of one particularly impressive tower.

Foggily, Zoccola remembered the long drive through the outskirts of Rabat. In the darkness he hadn't been able to keep track of where he was being taken, but it had been his impression that his uncommunicative escorts were taking him in circles, deliberately making it impossible for him to later retrace their route.

There had been a river crossing, he recalled, a short ferry boat ride, then another car journey which had come to an end at this place.

He tried the door. Much to his surprise, it opened, and he stepped out into a courtyard dominated by a waterless fountain.

"You are just in time for breakfast," someone said from his extreme left.

He turned and saw a white lawn table at which sat Maxim Kolnikov.

Incredulous that he had been kidnapped by the Soviets, Zoccola looked around for security men. The two of them appeared to be alone, though there was no telling who lurked beyond the courtyard door.

"Coffee?" Rather than wait for Zoccola's answer, Kolnikov poured the black liquid into a cup.

At last Zoccola managed to find his voice. "Where are we?" he asked, sounding foolish to himself.

"Pretty place, don't you think? It's called Chellah. It's really not so far from your hotel. Please sit down."

Utterly confused about the kidnapping, Zoccola wondered whether it was meant as some kind of test for him, whether he was simply a victim of the Russian's bizarre sense of humor, or whether Kolnikov might indeed be ready to turn. "Is this some sort of safe house?" he asked as he took a seat across from Kolnikov.

"You might say that. Your side doesn't know about it

and, more to the point, neither does mine."

"Will it be very long before I understand what's going on?"

"Not so long, really. I had to take some precautions, you see. If they weren't necessary I would not have subjected you to such an ordeal. But I could not take the chance that anyone would learn of our meeting here."

Zoccola began to have a glimmering about the Russian's motives, but he decided it best to let Kolnikov continue guiding the conversation.

"Is the coffee strong enough?" he asked.

Zoccola assured him that it was.

"I prepared it myself," he said with pride. "No Arab can make such coffee." He leaned closer to his involuntary guest, lowering his voice even though there was no one nearby to overhear him. "I wish to make a proposition to you."

"I'm listening," Zoccola replied quickly.

"When we last met in Agadir, you suggested that we might strike a deal."

Zoccola nodded. Maybe that dacha in Zagorsk was no longer as attractive a prospect as it once was, Zoccola thought.

"I have been thinking over your offer and I think that maybe we can work together. I would want some guarantees from your government first. I can do nothing without such guarantees."

"If you'd be a bit more specific . . ."

"Yes, yes, of course. Listen, I can be of great value to your people. I am worth a great deal of money to them."

"That remains to be seen."

"I will prove to you how important I can be. I will make you a favor. Unconditionally. If you are satisfied, we will talk again. Then we will talk about what *you* can give and what more I can give. Is that agreeable to you?''

"It sounds very interesting to me, but I'm not empowered to make commitments."

"I know exactly what you are empowered to do, Mr. Zoccola. It is not necessary to play cat and mouse with me."

"You seem to know more than I do," said Zoccola, smiling. "Tell me, what is this unconditional favor you've got in mind?"

"I will give you Ibrahim Brega."

"He's yours to give?" Zoccola asked casually, despite the sudden feelings of constriction in his throat.

"He does not think so, but he is. If you are persuasive with him perhaps he will tell you what happened to your satellite. That should be most illuminating, wouldn't you say?"

Zoccola agreed that it would.

"Now, Mr. Zoccola, some friends of mine will see to it that you are returned to your hotel. At seven this evening you will receive a phone call. A man will give you an address and there you shall find Mr. Brega."

It occurred to Zoccola that Kolnikov's offer might be a setup, that Kolnikov wasn't about to turn but was only pretending to do so. Brega could be a ruse, a deliberate sacrifice to make it appear as if Kolnikov had come over to the Americans. On the other hand, in cases like this there was never absolute proof. You had to go with your instincts and hope that somewhere down the line it paid off, while at the same time always hedging your bets.

Back at the Hilton, Zoccola spent the rest of the morning and most of the afternoon catching up on the news he'd missed during the last twelve hours. Hostilities had broken out along the Tunisian-Libyan border, but how serious these hostilities were was difficult to ascertain from the BBC and VOA broadcasts. The reports from the area where fighting was said to be going on were sketchy and full of contradictions. In the meantime, the government in Tunis was issuing statements dismissing the seriousness of the conflict by referring to it as an incident.

Incidents, however, had a way of turning into something more. Zoccola recalled the Gulf of Tonkin incident, which almost imperceptibly blossomed into the Vietnamese war.

Still, the authorities in Tunis were downplaying the seriousness of the border strife, maintaining that the situation was completely normal, so much so that the prime minister still planned to attend the Third World conference King Hassan II of Morocco had called for next week.

From Tripoli there was practically no information at all. According to the six o'clock BBC English language broadcast, a senior member of Qaddafi's Revolutionary Council denied that there was any problem whatsoever along the Libyan-Tunisian border, insisting that any report to the contrary was a fabrication. He added that Libya continued to be interested in a merger of the two nations if circumstances warranted, but the spokesman declined to detail just which circumstances he was referring to.

Unable to concentrate on the newspapers strewn about his room, Zoccola spent the hour before seven chain-smoking Camels and pacing around his bed.

At precisely seven o'clock the phone rang. One thing you had to give Maxim Kolnikov credit for: he was certainly punctual.

But it wasn't Kolnikov on the other end. The voice was completely unfamiliar.

"Tomorrow night, at eleven, the Palais Koutoubia, Rue Sanlucar, Tangier."

That was all the man said before hanging up.

Zoccola promptly put in a call to Drexell to apprise him of the situation.

"Are you familiar with the El Minzah?" Drexell asked him when he finally got on the line. "It's one of the better hotels in Tangier."

"I'll find it."

"Meet me there tomorrow at five. At the bar by the pool. I'm coming," Drexell said as an afterthought, "because it'll be easier to coordinate operations in Morocco than from four thousand miles away."

Zoccola didn't reply but sensed that the real reason for Drexell's arrival was that he would be more comfortable in the thick of action than manipulating things from behind the scenes.

Having nothing more to do for the next twenty odd hours, Zoccola decided to repair to the hotel bar downstairs. This time, he thought wryly, he would not be so ready to follow unknown Moroccan youths with messages.

The bar was not entirely empty but it might just as well have been. The few tourists and one sodden English businessman in the place didn't do much to lighten the atmosphere. Given the nature of his clientele it was no wonder that the middle-aged bartender looked as bored as he did.

But then Zoccola noticed some life come back into the man's eyes. He turned to see a young woman striding into the bar area. It took him a moment to realize that it was Adrienne Calenda. Her hair was tied back and hidden under a wide-brimmed cream-colored hat, and her eyes were barely visible behind expensive glasses which changed color depending on the light. Somehow looking more vulnerable than she had the day before, she was still an exceptional-looking woman who seemed perfectly aware of the effect she was creating.

She was alone, but in her case that didn't mean very much. There would soon be a husband or bodyguards with her.

She took a table in the back, but within sight of the bar, and ordered a white wine from the place's single waiter. Facing the doorway with an expectant air, she would glance down at her watch every now and again. The man—and there was no doubt in Zoccola's mind that it was a man—was late.

She was uneasy. She gave Zoccola the impression of someone who'd stopped smoking only a few days previously and hadn't yet discovered what she should do with her hands. She finished her white wine too quickly.

Zoccola told the bartender to buy her a drink on him. The bartender looked skeptical, then went to the end of the bar and whispered to the waiter. The latter proceeded to his customer and whispered to her. She raised her eyes and regarded Zoccola warily, then slowly shook her head. She wanted another white wine—but not on him.

Yesterday, Zoccola thought impatiently, there were bodyguards, today there were no bodyguards. Today there was an empty seat at her table.

No one who knew John Zoccola had ever credited him with restraint. Or patience, for that matter. When Adrienne Calenda next looked up toward the doorway, she found him blocking her view.

"I didn't invite you to sit down," she said coolly.

"I'm aware of that. But if I spent my life waiting for invitations from people I'd still be living in the Bronx."

"Maybe you ought to consider returning there."

"Where's your husband?"

"I don't think that's any business of yours," she replied, an extra layer of ice coating her words.

Zoccola smiled. "I can see we're going to get along splendidly. My name, by the way, is John Zoccola."

"It's a pleasure meeting you, Mr. Zoccola. But I'm afraid that we'll have to put off our getting acquainted until another time. I happen to be engaged at present."

Her voice had a certain lilt to it, a slightly breathless quality that Zoccola tended to associate with stage actresses. There was no accent at all; it was American, but sanitized. Zoccola had met people from California who talked this way.

"Tell you what; soon as your husband, or whoever it is you're meeting, comes along I'll be more than happy to surrender my chair, Miss Calenda."

She stiffened. "How did you know my name?"

"I even know that your husband's name is Adam Meureudu and that he's currently foreign minister of Indonesia."

"Very good," she said with a half-smile. "Now tell me something else, Mr. Zoccola—"

"Call me John, please."

"John. Do you always find out the names of every strange woman you're interested in before you meet them? Or do you concentrate more on their husbands?"

"I'd have to say about half and half," he replied.

He took out a cigarette, which elicited a yearning glance from her, confirming his guess that she'd stopped smoking only a few days before.

"It's hard. I tried kicking it half a dozen times myself. Never worked. I work under too much pressure."

"What is it that you do?" she asked in a neutral voice.

"Business," Zoccola answered quickly. "I'm a consultant. A company gets in trouble they call on me, ask me for my opinion."

"Are you often correct?"

"I'm still under contract, so somebody must like me. And what about you? You enjoy playing the role of foreign minister's wife?"

"Do I detect a certain disdain in your voice?"

"Only interest."

"Let's just say that it's a role that provides me with many unusual opportunities."

"You get to meet a lot of well-connected people."

"That's right. Tell me, John, are you well-connected?"

"Do I look well-connected?"

For the first time she allowed herself to smile. "Yes, I think you do. After a while you begin to recognize the type. Now, I'm afraid you're going to have to excuse yourself."

"You said that to me before."

"This time it's different," she said, vaguely amused.

Looking back toward the door to the bar, Zoccola understood what she was talking about. Standing there were the two bodyguards he'd seen accompanying her yesterday; neither of them seemed pleased to see him.

"My husband," said Adrienne, "has a formidable reputation."

"In regard to you?"

"If it were just me I would not be calling his reputation formidable."

She began to get up from the table, and Zoccola did also. "Are you staying in Rabat for long?" he asked.

"No, not very long."

"Do me a favor, will you?"

"What's that?" she asked, more serious than amused.

"Next time let me buy you a drink."

"Will there be a next time?" That faint smile reappeared again, then quickly vanished.

"I think so."

"Maybe you're right," she conceded.

He watched as she moved toward the door. He liked the way her legs moved.

The two bodyguards didn't say a word to her, but they gave her—and Zoccola—looks that showed how angry they were. Zoccola suddenly had the impression that these men weren't protecting her but rather were watching her for her husband. It was as though she weren't a wife so much as a captive whose most rebellious act was to go to a bar and have a drink by herself.

He'd been right about her waiting for someone. But he'd been wrong about her wanting that someone to show up.

13

Prior to his departure for Morocco, Drexell asked to consult with the President once more. And this time it was a private meeting, with no one else present in the Oval Office when they met at 10:49 P.M. Whether the President was taping the conversation, as many of his predecessors in office had, Drexell didn't know, but even here the President characteristically refrained from making any rash statements.

Creighton Turner's eyes were ringed with black and his skin had a sallow look. He tapped his fingers continuously on the desktop and from time to time an abstracted expression came over his face, as though his mind was somewhere far away. How did this man get elected? Drexell thought suddenly in wonderment. But then, Drexell rarely watched the television so he was no authority on the subject of electoral campaigns.

"How is it out there, Bill?"

"Fairly warm. Hasn't cooled off much."

Actually it was a close, hot night, but even in the mat-

ter of the weather Drexell tended toward understate-
ment.

"I'd hoped to get away. You know my friend Dodge
Lewellyn? He and his wife invited us sailing off New-
port for a couple of days."

Drexell had met Dodge. He was a multimillionaire
who had once invented a kind of widget that made
bombs explode with more efficient impact, and he had
somehow worked himself into the chairmanship of a
company which manufactured cosmetic goods.

"Well, you still might, Mr. President, if this whole
thing cools down soon."

The President appeared dubious. "I talked to the
Soviet watch desk over at State. They've been analyzing
that major statement the Russians came out with. They
don't think it amounts to a hill of beans. The consensus
over there still seems to be that Kadiyev is more or less
in charge. What's your view on that?"

As it happened, Drexell was so preoccupied by consolidating operations in North Africa that he hadn't had
the time to consider the chain of command in Moscow.
"I'd go with their assessment until you get information
telling you different," he said neutrally.

"I've decided that, after Rudnitsky's stonewalling, it
makes sense to try the hot line. I wanted you here while I
talk to him. We can discuss the North African situation
afterward."

Drexell nodded, and the President buzzed his secretary. "Would you mind sending Bailey in?"

Bailey Myers, an interpreter on loan from State, had
spent a year at Lomonosov University in Moscow studying the Bolshevik Revolution, and was as fluent in Russian as any native American possibly could be. A sober-
looking young man, obviously in awe of his role, he

entered the office and quickly took a seat at the opposite end of the room. A single black phone with six extensions rested on the small round table in front of him.

Up until this administration, the so-called hot line between the White House and Kremlin was actually a telex. It was reasoned that if the leaders of the two superpowers had the opportunity to speak directly to each other in the heat of crisis, they might end up hardening their positions and exacerbating the situation. Communication by telex was to give each man time to reflect on what he wished to say. But the current President, with Soviet approval, had decided that this risk was preferable to the indirect method of the previous system.

"When I tell you to, Bailey, pick up," the President said. To Drexell he added, "I'm going to put this on conference so you'll be able to hear what Kadiyev has to say. That is, if we succeed in getting him on the line."

The President and Bailey picked up their phones, and after several minutes of confused dialogue between the President, his interpreter, several baffled functionaries in the Kremlin, and their interpreters, a connection was finally established.

But the connection was not with Kadiyev, but rather with the President of the Supreme Soviet, Vladimir Pomorov, whose post was an entirely honorary one. The Supreme Soviet was nothing more than a rubber stamp parliament.

Pomorov apologized for the absence of the First Secretary and the Premier. "They are involved in urgent consultations," he explained.

"When can I speak directly to the First Secretary?"

"If he is available, Mr. President, perhaps later today or early this evening, Moscow time."

"That is not satisfactory to us."

There was an extended pause at the other end. "I am very sorry, I can only convey my sincerest apology to you."

"What could be more urgent than a call from the President of the United States?" Turner said angrily. "What if I had news that nuclear weapons had been launched in the direction of Moscow and Leningrad?"

Drexell was disturbed by the President's wild statement. Turner was plainly showing his exhaustion. Even without translation, Pomorov's voice betrayed his anxiety. "That is not, however, the reason you called, is it?"

"No, of course that's not why I called. I called, first of all, to find out whether Alexei Kadiyev is in fact the First Secretary."

"I give you my assurances, Mr. President, that his position is not in any dispute."

Drexell didn't fail to note the subtle ambiguity in his words.

Neither did the President: "Again I am asking you—is Mr. Kadiyev the First Secretary?"

"I believe that the statement issued by the Communist Party of the Soviet Union yesterday makes clear that Alexei Kadiyev enjoys its full confidence and support."

Exasperated, the President turned the conversation to the subject of the movement of the Black Sea Fleet.

"It is true, Mr. President," Pomorov replied, "that our deployment of our fleet in the Mediterranean area has changed in the last several days, but may I assure you that this is routine and represents no threat to the territorial integrity of any nation. I do wish to say, on behalf of the Soviet government, that it is with great alarm that we view the unnecessary buildup of forces on the part of your country and your NATO allies. To place your armies on a higher alert is a step that we regard as unjustified by events and, most certainly, as an act of provocation. If you retain your forces on a war footing, the Soviet Union, in consultation with her allies, may be obliged to retaliate.''

The President seemed almost distracted as he listened to the translation of Pomorov's well-modulated admonition. "Just what is the nature of this retaliation?" Turner asked when the Russian's message had been conveyed.

"I am not at liberty to say. It would, however, depend on the prevailing situation at the time. But please do not misunderstand me, Mr. President. Just as you are anxious to maintain the peace, so are we. We do not wish confrontation nor do we invite it.''

With a curtness that Drexell was sure wasn't lost on Pomorov, the President put an end to the conversation: "Please tell the First Secretary," he barked, "whether he turns out to be Mr. Kadiyev or not, that I am prepared to talk with him—seriously—about these matters at any time. I expect a call from him within twenty-four hours. Good night, President Pomorov.''

The final translation finished, Turner and Bailey hung up, and the President turned back to Drexell. "Well, what did you think?''

"I think we don't know any more than we did before —except that the shakeup is still continuing. I suspect that there's really no one in charge and that the jockeying for power is in full swing. Right now, there's probably no one aside from Pomorov who has the authority to take the call.''

"A goddamn fuck-up," muttered the President.

Then, suddenly conscious of the interpreter's presence in the room, he said, "Thank you, Bailey, you may go now."

The translator left the Oval Office as swiftly as he had come in.

There was a protracted silence during which the President was either lost in thought or had simply blanked out.

"Excuse me, Mr. President, may we take up the matter of Operation Undercross? I won't be able to discuss it with you after I leave tonight."

"Undercross? I thought we decided to put that on the back burner."

The secret plan referred to by the President was an updated version of "Triple Squeeze," a plan that had originally been designed by the French for the purpose of overthrowing Qaddafi. As its name suggested, Triple Squeeze consisted of three separate operations which relied on ships, marines, and Libyan emigré forces to be used against the Qaddafi regime. There was, in addition, a fourth aspect of this plan—a fourth squeeze—which was based on the use of the U.S. arsenal of nuclear weapons stockpiled on NATO bases in Turkey. The plan called for the use of these nuclear weapons only in the event that the Soviet Union decided to resort to all-out war to maintain the Libyan dictator in power.

Undercross, the U.S.'s current version of Triple Squeeze, was a more modest plan which involved neither the direct use of U.S. combat forces nor a major naval assault. Its objective was not to bring down Qaddafi (though no one would've minded if this did occur), but rather to cause enough havoc in his country to prevent him from invading Tunisia.

Undercross, like Triple Squeeze, did depend on the use of Libyan emigré and mercenary forces. While

American advisers would accompany them, the idea was to minimize American exposure in combat. One of the emigré forces' principal targets was the destruction of the installation from which, Drexell was almost sure, the antisatellite missile had been launched several days previously.

If Undercross ruled out American ground forces, it didn't, however, necessarily rule out the judicious deployment of U.S. air power.

"We had put Undercross on the shelf, Mr. President. But present circumstances demand a fresh look at it. I've been in touch with my agent in the area and he confirms that an invasion of Libyan armed forces is under way in the south of Tunisia. With the other things happening in the area, there may be a major shift in power in North Africa away from the U.S. If we don't do anything."

"Well, Bill," the President said softly, as if he were trying to calm the other man, "I've spoken both to the Tunisian ambassador and to sources at Langley and they both say that it's a limited operation and that we don't want to overreact. It's one thing to shoot down a couple of MiG's over the Gulf of Sidra; it's quite another to sponsor an army of exile troops."

The incident the President referred to had taken place in 1982 over water that Qaddafi claimed as Libyan, a claim disputed by the U.S.

"Nonetheless, sir, I urge you to at least let me institute a modified form of Undercross. I believe events are moving in a direction where we may need it. I've been in contact with the Libyan emigrés, and it would require only a day or two to organize them into commando units. By carrying out sabotage in Libya itself we might succeed in buying ourselves some time elsewhere in the region."

"It could be a hell of a mess if word got out that we were in any way involved," the President warned.

"You'll be covered. I mean to get the men in and out before Qaddafi knows what the hell happened."

"Let me sleep on it and I'll get back to you before tomorrow night."

"I repeat, sir: using the emigrés may mean the difference between losing our North African allies or not."

"Well, I'm sending Jeffrey up to the Hill tomorrow to request emergency military aid packages for both Tunisia and Morocco. I think this is one we can get. As soon as it's approved we're going to start airlifting them as many advanced fighters and tanks as we can lay our hands on."

"That *will* be of great value, but to save the region, I'll need your personal approval for Undercross."

"Don't pressure me, please, Bill," the President warned as he rose from his chair. The interview had obviously come to an end. "I told you I'll sleep on it and get back to you on it. Now, tell me how you're getting over there."

"The VC-137 has been placed at my disposal," he explained, referring to the military version of the Boeing 747. The VC-137 was provided with a full complement of communications equipment.

"You're lucky to be getting it. You might have been stuck with the KC-135. The VC is a lot more comfortable to sleep on, and it has windows too. Always nice to have a view, I find," the President said, shaking Drexell's hand and escourting him to the door of the Oval Office

As he left the President, however, Drexell was not especially interested in the advantages of the VC-137. Rather, Drexell was only interested in getting the President's sanction for Undercross as soon as possible, for the truth was that Drexell had already set the plan in motion, and if the President ultimately decided against the operation there would be all hell to pay. The Libyans, with their own territory secure, would be able to continue consolidating their gains in Tunisia while still retaining the capability of knocking U.S. spy satellites out of the sky any time they chose. Not only would the U.S. be losing an ally, but it wouldn't know about it until it was too late. Of course, the chief beneficiaries would be the Soviets, who, through Libya, would have enormously increased their influence in the area.

14

As the President had said, the VC-137 was equipped with comfortable sleeping facilities as well as windows, but Drexell had little inclination either to sleep or to watch the North Atlantic in the middle of the night.

The extensive communications facilities, however, were of great use to him, and he directed his aide, Steven Cavanaugh, to try to reach first Lisker and then Hahn. Having earlier arranged to meet Zoccola at the Tangier hotel, Drexell didn't need to communicate with him now. It was not yet seven in the morning Moroccan time, and Lisker was sleeping when Cavanaugh called him.

"This is Clausewitz," Drexell said. "How do you feel this morning?"

"Fine," Lisker replied groggily.

"I trust you're sufficiently articulate to tell me what's happening there," Drexell ordered. Lisker had arrived only the day before in Fez, the ancient capital of Morocco, having spent the last three days driving through the countryside north from Agadir in an anonymous pick-up truck. The incident involving the Russian trawler over, Drexell had asked him to take the scenic route to Fez. Valuing his discerning eye, he hoped that Lisker would have some useful observations to make regarding the state of affairs in the Moroccan interior. And indeed he did. The previous day Lisker had summed up his impressions in a terse telegram that he intended to elaborate on later: "Natives restless. Rioting imminent."

Lisker's arrival in Fez coincided with the unexpected announcement by King Hassan II that he was convoking an emergency meeting of Third World nations. While he had not made his reasons perfectly clear, it appeared that Hassan was attempting to mount international support for his regime at a time when his domestic position seemed particularly vulnerable, what with Polisario guerrilla incursions and an imperiled economy threatening his rule. With the Algerians backing the Polisario on one side, and the Libyans threatening the sovereignty of Tunisia—the only other pro-Western state in North Africa—the emergency Third World conference was seen by other leaders in the area as the act of a desperate but very shrewd man. Hassan believed that by assembling hundreds of leaders, foreign ministers, and titular heads of state he could both shore up his reputation in the international community and prove to his foreign adversaries that Morocco was not without supporters in the world. Moreover, he felt that the attendant publicity would evoke in the West—particularly in America—an outpouring of sympathy for him that might translate into money and arms for his country.

It was not for nothing that Hassan had managed to survive for so many years on the throne of Morocco.

It was to monitor the unstable situation in Fez, where

the conference was to take place, that Drexell had dispatched Lisker to the ancient capital.

Lisker was now more than half awake and quite articulate. "From what I can gather," Lisker said, "the main concern here is how many countries intend to send representatives and just what kind of representatives will come. The people around the throne are acting like nervous hostesses before a party, and there's real fear that the Saudis and the Kuwaitis and the other Gulf states won't show. And they're the ones with the cash. Or there's concern that they'll send low-ranking princes or ministers without portfolio. Well over one hundred countries have been invited, but I still have no word on how many will actually show up. But I'll tell you this much, I don't think the security here is worth a damn."

"Keep working on it," Drexell said, his voice now gruffly supportive. "But I expect you in Tangier this afternoon at five in the courtyard of the El Minzah Hotel. We'll have some important matters to discuss there."

Lisker assured him that he'd be there.

The conversation ended, Drexell instructed Cavanaugh to try to contact Hahn. For several minutes Cavanaugh continued to adjust the transmitter to all frequencies on which they were supposed to be monitoring Hahn, but all he got were fitful bursts of static. "I'm afraid that we can't reach him, sir," Cavanaugh said.

"Either that or he's not where he's supposed to be," Drexell said gloomily.

"We can try again in a little while. The problem might simply be atmospheric conditions."

"I doubt it. He was receiving messages this morning, wasn't he?"

"Yes sir."

''So we can only hope our men find him before the Libyans or the Mullah's boys do.''

The men Drexell referred to were in the secret Undercross commando unit, currently consisting of fifty-five men. The commandos were mostly exiled Libyan mercenaries, although there were two American advisers, code-named Shaw and Hunt, attached to the group.

He'd already alerted the secret force to find Hahn in Medenine and prepare for a strike despite the President's indecisiveness.

This was the only reason he'd assumed command of Triad and not retired to his home in Tappahannock, Virginia—he'd been assured he could act with relatively full autonomy. If the President tied his hands, that autonomy wouldn't mean a damn. Under present circumstances, therefore, he saw no option but to exercise the autonomy he had been promised, despite the lack of formal Presidential authority.

He leaned back, staring out of the oval window to his right; the jet was speeding toward the new day and already a trace of sunlight was visible, defining a thick layer of cumulus against the slate-gray sky.

Tomorrow, he would deal with Undercross.

Today, he would be the mysterious Mr. Ibrahim Brega.

15

The Palais Koutoubia was particularly crowded this night, filled with spirited gamblers and drinkers whose eyes were so concentrated on the roulette wheel and the blackjack tables that they scarcely took in the lavish display of flesh that was being offered them as one belly dancer after another sent her midriff into intriguing contortions.

Lisker watched all this, thinking how curious it was that in times of crisis, when the world was mired in depression or when war threatened, people chose to throw themselves into a frenzy of undisciplined behavior. The poor took to drink and complained, and the rich came to places like this and squandered hundreds of thousands of dollars, lire, francs, marks, and kronen, all in futile efforts to convince themselves that they still held some power over fate.

Lisker's attitude, born of a resolutely conservative background, was that nothing was yet out of control, that the law of entropy was not universal. It was not inevitable that everything should wind down, lose energy, and degenerate into chaos and anarchy. He looked on these people as children who would never grow up and who richly deserved to be punished by being made to work for a living.

But tonight Lisker was too preoccupied by other concerns to really care about the state of world morality. He was almost entirely focused on the fact that they were finally to confront Ibrahim Brega, the man he'd been pursuing on and off since his arrival in Morocco.

That afternoon at their meeting in the courtyard of the elegant El Minzah Hotel, Drexell, looking drawn from lack of sleep but obviously enlivened by once again being back in the fray, had personally taken command of the Brega kidnapping. Besides Zoccola and Lisker, he'd also enlisted the small contingent of trusted operatives he could rely on in Tangier.

These operatives were now circulating through the club, pretending to be absorbed in the rotation of the roulette wheel and the throw of cards in games of Twenty-One. At a signal from either Lisker or Zoccola they would instantly move according to a preestablished plan.

In the meantime, Drexell was sitting outside in an anonymous-looking 1980 Ford sedan parked immediately in front of the Koutoubia.

The success of the operation depended almost entirely on Zoccola and Lisker, for they were the only two to have actually laid eyes on Brega. Since he might appear in disguise, they watched the gambling room with nervous alertness.

There was no sign of him during the early hours of the evening, but at five minutes to eleven the agent nearest the door glanced up to see a man who perfectly matched the one photograph of the mysterious Mr. Brega available to U.S. intelligence. He signaled the other operatives with a slight tilt of the head and then, casually, began following Brega as he advanced in the direction of the gaming tables. With him was another man whose identity and relationship to Brega were unclear to the observers.

To Lisker, standing near one of the card tables, there was no question that this was Brega. Except for trimming his beard since their near encounter in the Agadir hotel lobby, he had done nothing to alter his appearance. Either he anticipated no danger or else felt assured that there was no threat he couldn't effectively handle.

When he and his companion reached the roulette table they separated, Brega remaining where he was while the other man vanished into the crowd. When the other man reappeared he held an impressive number of chips, which the two of them immediately began to bet. To all appearances, Lisker mused, Brega was spending the money the Russians must have paid him to sabotage the satellite.

Let him enjoy himself while he could, Lisker thought. The opportunity won't come his way again.

How much enjoyment Brega was receiving, though, was difficult to tell. From the baleful expression on his face and from the curses that spilled from his lips, he appeared to be losing heavily.

Independently, each of those watching him saw that it was impossible to move in on Brega so long as he remained at the tables. And he evidently had no intention of leaving them until he recouped his losses. This didn't appear about to happen soon, and impatience began to gnaw at both Zoccola and Lisker as they realized there was nothing they could do to speed things up.

Eventually Brega realized that it was senseless to continue staking ever greater denominations of chips in hopes that his luck would change, and started to leave the table. His companion, however, a perpetually smiling man who had been faring better than Brega, seemed noticeably reluctant to leave, and for several minutes it appeared as though he would stay put. Lisker realized that it would make the snatch that much easier if he did.

In the end, however, the companion agreed to call it a night and together the two started for the exit.

As the two men proceeded through the club the operatives followed along behind, maintaining a discreet distance. Brega continued to look preoccupied, apparently in contemplation of the night's losses.

There were still too many people about for Lisker's liking. In particular, half a dozen richly dressed people were milling near the doorway, conversing volubly in Italian. In addition, there were two doormen at the entrance, plus a burly man incongruously outfitted in black tie who probably acted as a security guard.

Brega, his friend trailing right behind, pushed his way through the Italians. Just as he stepped out onto the street Lisker acted, signaling the two agents closest to Brega to proceed with the snatch.

They moved expertly, jostling Brega as if by accident, then separated him from his friend and hustled him toward Drexell's Ford. His friend stood rooted to the spot for several moments, his mouth gaping open in surprise. Then, regaining the use of his voice, he shouted and started out after Brega, only to find his way cut off by yet a third agent.

The rear door of the Ford swung open and Brega was thrust inside before he could cry out. The door slammed shut and with a great shriek of rubber on pavement, the car sped down the Rue Sanlucar and was quickly gone from sight.

Just outside the club, Lisker and Zoccola pretended to be interested observers, nothing more. Events had occurred with such swiftness that most of the witnesses, the excitable Italians among them, were unclear as to what it was they had seen.

In the meantime, Brega's friend was stamping his feet and cornering anyone he could to help him. The security guard came out of the club to see what all the commotion was about, but he seemed rather bored by the friend's protests, and soon returned inside.

"It looks like a success," Lisker remarked when Zoccola came up beside him.

"Maxim was right on target," Zoccola replied.

Rather than risk being seen together for any length of time, the two men went their separate ways. They would link up again in an hour's time at a safe house located inside the old city walls.

The safe house was actually a couple of cold rooms on the third floor of a narrow building which occupied a corner of the Socco Chico, the small marketplace. Even at this late hour, long-haired youths, seemingly left over from the 1960's, sat in cafés, dazedly consuming mint teas, their long silences and indifferent posture testifying to hours of kif smoking. Youngsters in the square hawked drugs, shoeshines, and their sisters in a bewildering variety of languages. In another country their parents would have made sure they were home in bed. In Morocco there were no parents for children like these, who were left to fend for themselves.

Lisker made his way to a narrow, sagging building in the corner of the square where he was received by a prematurely aged woman with round cheeks and flashing eyes. He was led up two flights of rickety stairs to the second landing. The woman indicated a closed door and returned down the stairs.

Lisker paused a moment. He knew that, according to plan, Brega would have been treated well up to this point. Once he was relaxed, he, Lisker, the Task Force's communications expert, was to apply his own methods.

He stepped into the room, and, without glancing at Drexell, pulled up a chair and leaned across the table, his eyes fixed on the apparently indifferent prisoner. This, Lisker thought, is the man who could tell them how the Soviets knocked out their satellite. And with this evidence, Drexell could force the President to take a more decisive role.

In a moment Drexell arose from his chair at the table and gave Lisker the ghost of a smile.

Lisker was also smiling now, but it was an unearthly, skeletal rictus meant to unnerve. He settled back in his chair, rocking it gently, saying nothing.

"He's not interested in money, it seems," Drexell said. "And he doesn't seem to appreciate our considerate treatment. I think we need some real persuasion here, Jim." Drexell looked paternally at both men and quietly left the room.

Brega waited for Lisker to do something and began squirming in his chair, avoiding Lisker's unrelenting gaze.

Suddenly Lisker sprang up, and in a motion too quick for Brega to register, tipped over Brega's chair and sent him sprawling backward. His head smacked against the floor, making him cry out.

Then Lisker pulled him up bodily, dropping him back into the chair. With his right hand, he grabbed hold of Brega's chin and forced his head back.

Still not recovered from the blow to his head, Brega raised his eyes imploringly toward Lisker but, aside from a groan, he made no sound.

"It is no problem for me, Mr. Brega, to break your neck. Do you understand?"

To emphasize his words he tipped the other's head back another quarter of an inch, exposing the white of his neck.

He released him and just as abruptly seized hold of his left hand and broke his little finger.

Brega screamed, nearly jerking out of the chair. Tears came to his eyes.

"That's to show you that I do not make empty threats," Lisker said, in a very soft voice. "I intend to continue breaking your fingers, one by one, until you begin to tell me what I need to know. If you still continue to defy me, then I will simply have to begin on other parts of your anatomy."

Brega was still gasping. All at once, he doubled over and began to vomit.

Lisker watched him indifferently.

When he was through, Lisker asked, "Who hired you to sabotage the satellite tracking system at El Jadida?"

Brega said nothing. Lisker took hold of his left hand and snapped the middle finger. This made Brega retch again, but all he could do was dry heave, as he'd already emptied the contents of his stomach moments before.

He mumbled something Lisker didn't catch.

"Say it again."

"A man, he comes and pays me in cash. Once a week I meet with him, always at some different place. He says his name is Nikita.''

Lisker assumed Nikita was a code name.

"Russian?"

Brega nodded. The blood had drained from his face, and his breathing was shallow. He forced himself to keep from looking at his hands. Lisker noticed that the two fractured fingers had swollen and taken on a bright scarlet color.

Outside the door, Lisker suddenly became aware of a number of voices, Drexell's among them. He couldn't identify the others, but all he cared about was extracting as much information from the prisoner as possible.

"Yes, Russian, I think."

"What did he look like?"

"Thin, mustache, hard eyes."

Since Nikita was probably only a go-between, a description wasn't of the greatest importance. The main thing was that they had gotten direct testimony of Soviet involvement, something that had been lacking up to this point.

"How long have you been working for Nikita?"

"Five months. Five and a half months, I think."

"Do you know what happened to the satellite? To Secsat DV-2?"

Brega was silent until Lisker took hold of his hand again, then he shrieked. Lisker didn't bother breaking another finger; he didn't need to. As Brega continued speaking, the voices outside the room grew louder; an argument seemed to be developing. It began to annoy Lisker, distracting him from the business at hand.

"I know what happened," Brega admitted, his own voice barely audible.

"Tell me."

"Missile."

"Whose missile?"

"East German."

"Where was it launched from?"

Another silence. Lisker simply focused his eyes on Brega's hands.

"Libya, I think. A place called ORTAG."

"How did you find this out? From Nikita?"

Brega shook his head. "Not from Nikita."

At that moment the door flew open and Drexell appeared.

He glanced at Brega and then his gaze fell on the pool of vomit at his feet. "Have you got anything?" he asked Lisker.

"We're making definite progress, Mr. Brega and I."

"Unfortunately, we'll have to give him up," he said, dead serious.

"What the hell—"

"I've got a fellow name of Casin out there, Douglas Casin."

"CIA station chief here?"

"That's right. We also got somebody else named Lawrence Pryor, a Princeton boy from the looks of him. He says he represents the NSC."

"What's the National Security Council doing interfering with our show?"

"That's exactly what I'd like to know. But they have authorization from the President to take him with them."

Brega was looking from one man to the other, trying to understand the conversation.

"Where do they intend to take him?"

"The security center of the Moroccan national police. Somebody evidently leaked word to the Moroccans that we have him," Drexell said, nodding to Brega, "they want in."

Pryor and Casin came into the small room and asked Drexell if the prisoner was ready for transfer.

When they saw Brega, they were appalled.

"Who gave you authorization to treat this man this way?" Pryor demanded.

Drexell allowed that he did. "And he was beginning to cooperate before you gentlemen came along."

"God, it stinks in here," said Casin.

"He's your stink now," Lisker said, looking at the intruders with murderous intensity. In a moment the two men and their new prisoner had left the room, and Drexell and Lisker followed them out. They found Zoccola and five other men waiting in a room down the hall. The latter were obviously expecting instructions from Casin while Zoccola was busy ignoring them.

"What's happening here?" Lisker demanded of Drexell. "They put every CIA asset they have in Tangier on this case?"

"That's what it looks like," Drexell said.

Casin decided to leave in two teams. The first would descend to the main square of the Socco Chico with a decoy disguised as Brega, while the real Brega would be spirited away out the back door of the building and into an adjoining alleyway, where a second car would be waiting for them.

It was still dark at three-fifteen in the morning, the square almost completely deserted save for the occasional stray cat. Even the long-haired youths, with their minds hovering within clouds of kif, had gone home.

The first team, consisting of three of the CIA operatives and the decoy, moved with admirable efficiency. Lisker watched them from the window as a black Renault pulled up, the men quickly got inside, and the car did an abrupt U-turn and sped through the market gate into the new city.

A slitlike window in the rear wall allowed Lisker to see what was occurring in the alleyway in back.

Zoccola came to watch beside him. Drexell, however, was too angry to watch. "I've got to get to the President on this," he said through clenched teeth. "This situation is intolerable, every son of a bitch stepping on every other goddamn son of a bitch's toes." The others had never seen Drexell so openly furious.

Lisker saw a Mercedes idling below. It was large enough and the alley small enough that it virtually filled the width of the passageway. For several moments that was all they saw. Then the second team, which included Casin and Pryor, appeared, their footsteps echoing off the high walls of the alley.

Casin opened the rear door of the Mercedes while the operative took hold of Brega's arm to propel him inside. Pryor got in at the wheel.

Then Lisker heard the sound of gunshots, greatly amplified by the acoustics of the tangled streets. Brega stiffened eloquently, his eyes clouding, and blood flooded the coils of his black hair. Then he collapsed, tumbling into the back seat of the Mercedes.

"They've hit him," Zoccola muttered in amazement. "They've goddamn hit him."

He didn't know for certain who the assassins might be, but he naturally assumed they were Soviet agents. Drexell rushed to the slit in the wall and peered out.

By this time Brega had been pushed all the way inside and the vehicle was in motion.

There were no further shots, but no more were necessary, Lisker thought, as the Mercedes disappeared around a corner. Brega was dead or critically injured. Either way they had lost their man.

• • •

TELEPHONE CONVERSATION
TRANSCRIPT   JULY 28, 1986

Call Initiated by White House
Logged in at 1:42 a.m., EDT

President: I heard you lost Brega.

Drexell: He was hit four hours ago, about 3 A.M.
    He's in critical condition, not expected to re-
    cover. There were too many people in the act.
    CIA, NSC, the Moroccans. That's how the
    Russians heard about it.

President: There was a fuck-up somewhere along
    the line and I take the blame for it. I'll try and
    see that it doesn't happen again.

Drexell: You get too many people, Mr. President,
    leaks are unavoidable. Triad just can't per-
    form under those circumstances.

President: I understand. But did you get anything
    from him?

Drexell: Number one, we have confirmation of
    direct Soviet involvement. The contact who
    paid Brega off was Soviet. Two, we have con-
    firmation of the base where the missile that
    killed Secsat came from. The East German in-
    stallation in Libya.

President: Very interesting.

Drexell: I think that if you do authorize Under-cross, that base would make a perfect target.

President: All right, Bill, but confine our actions to that.

Drexell: Excellent.

President: And keep our asses covered.

Drexell: Absolutely.

President: One other thing that might be of interest to you.

Drexell: What's that, sir?

President: I've spoken to Rameau in Paris and he agreed that the French do have a special responsibility in the area, Morocco and Tunisia having once been theirs. They also have troops committed in Chad, and there's no reason they can't use the Legion and the Force de Frappe in Tunisia.

Drexell: No reason at all. Are you planning any action on the part of our forces?

President: I'm considering it. Kadiyev still hasn't gotten back to me since our conversation the day before yesterday. I'm going to have to wake Rudnitsky up again and see what the hell he has to say. The deployment of the Black Sea Fleet off the Gulf of Sidra has me especially worried. Tass keeps saying it's all routine maneuvering and refueling exercises, but you know what kind of bullshit that is. In any case, whatever's going on you can be sure I'll reply in equal measure.

Drexell: I'm sure you will, Mr. President.

President: I'm sorry about Brega, but at least you got what you wanted from him. Good night.

Drexell: Good night, Mr. President.

Conversation terminated at 1:58 a.m., EDT.

16

The sound of rifle shots echoed against the walls of the stone courtyard in which Hahn and Jamal Azhmeh sat eating days-old pita bread. It was the only food Hahn had had since the preceding afternoon and he felt fortunate enough to have it that he could overlook its stale, hard tastelessness.

Azhmeh had assured him that the courtyard, which was a long way from their original starting place at Azhmeh's shop, would be a sufficiently secure hiding place until dark. Then they would have to move again. Life had been a repetition of running and hiding ever since Hahn had arrived in Medenine, where the djbella-clad soldiers of the Al-Jihad were in virtual control of the city.

For the last two days he and Azhmeh had been scrambling from one abandoned house to the next in search of sanctuary, keeping to the doorways, embracing the shadows, dropping to the pavement at the sudden appearance of a foot patrol or personnel carrier advancing through the narrow, rutted streets. And no matter where they went, no matter what time of day or night it happened to be, there was always the sound of small arms fire.

The rifle shots were a routine by now. Hahn was never able to say whether they were being fired by snipers loyal to the Tunisian regime or by the Al-Jihad. It was probable, however, that many people were being taken out and executed. Azhmeh believed that a proscription list had been drawn up for Medenine and, no doubt, for every other city and town of any significance in the country. All those men and women who might be expected to resist the Libyan-backed fundamentalists would undoubtedly be on it.

Nor was there any question in Azhmeh's mind—or Hahn's—that should they be found they themselves would be ruthlessly interrogated, tortured, and then lined up against a wall and shot.

Their only hope was to escape the city before this eventuality occurred. They were to head out of Medenine by nightfall in hopes of linking up with the Undercross operatives dispatched by Drexell to extricate them from the area. Hahn knew them only by their code names, Hunt and Shaw.

As all the arrangements to meet them had been made two days before through a series of coded messages transmitted by Azhmeh's radio, he had no way of determining whether the originally agreed-upon plan of action was still on. In a situation as confused as this, last-minute changes were more the rule than the exception.

The radio, however, had simply been too awkward and heavy to carry with them, and so without any means to confirm the link-up, Hahn now had to rely on pure luck.

Clearly it was going to be impossible to track down

the Mullah. It was all that he and the tanner could do to stay alive. Moreover, they had no indication exactly where the Mullah was. His voice was everywhere, though, emanating from every radio, and at such a high volume that it almost drowned out the monotonous staccato of the gunfire. His message, hour after hour, was practically the same: The faithful should rise up and overthrow their corrupt oppressors and restore to their country the rule of God and the Prophet, and all those who sacrificed themselves for this cause would be guaranteed a place in paradise. On the other hand, those who dared oppose the justice of God, as dispensed by His holy forces, should expect only death as a reward. And death for the unbelievers would not be accompanied by any reservation in paradise.

However, while these exhortations were broadcast regularly, there was no way to ascertain whether they were coming from a transmitter inside Tunisian territory or from Libya, whether they were live or taped in advance of the Libyan incursion.

In addition to the Mullah's hourly ravings, delivered in a hoarse, high-pitched voice, the same transmitter was broadcasting specific orders to the captive populace. These orders, issued by the "ruling tribunal of the new Islamic state of Libya-Tunisia," an otherwise unidentified governing body, concerned virtually every aspect of life. Women were to adopt the veil and to eschew wearing slacks or short dresses or any other clothes that might be regarded as unseemly. Gambling and the consumption of alcoholic beverages were prohibited. And all civil and criminal disputes were henceforth to be settled by Koranic law, which was subject to the interpretation of the clerics. It was not specified which clerics these were, but it was to be assumed that they were appointed by the tribunal. And until the area

was completely "pacified" martial law was to obtain
and a curfew, from six o'clock in the evening until four
the following morning, was to be rigorously observed.
All those venturing out on the streets between those
hours were liable to be arrested or simply shot on sight,
the radio declared.

Actually, from all that Hahn could see, those who
ventured out during the daylight hours were every bit as
likely to be shot as well. For himself and Azhmeh, in
fact, darkness was preferred, for much of the night was
without benefit of revealing illumination. The electricity
functioned erratically, and the street lights had a habit
of sputtering and dying, only to come back to life again
without any warning ten minutes or an hour later.

Although Hahn was now disguised in a robe and bur-
noose that Azhmeh had provided, he was doubtful as to
the safety of the courtyard they had taken refuge in, this
in spite of Azhmeh's conviction that they were safe until
darkness. While the constant rattle of automatic fire
didn't alarm him, the repeated cries of men and women
being dragged from their homes and carried away had
Hahn unnerved. It was a sound he didn't think he could
ever get used to.

Having finished his bread, he decided to explore their
surroundings. It was best, he felt, to find other means of
egress in case they were compelled to make a swift
retreat. Azhmeh, however, seemed not to care about
establishing safeguards. If it were up to him he would
remain huddled in the corner, drowsily enjoying the sun
for the remainder of the afternoon.

The courtyard was small and rectangular and pro-
tected by high white stone walls. At the opposite end
was a high arched door ornamented by a series of
brightly colored concentric circles.

Hahn put his ear to the door, but he could hear

nothing. Then he pushed against it. It swung open easily to reveal a courtyard that in every respect duplicated the one he'd just stepped out of except that this one wasn't empty. Instead, it was filled with bodies.

There must have been a score of them, mostly men, but there were at least half a dozen women too, one of them barely out of her teens. Their postures in death suggested that they'd been trying to find a way out when they were cut down. Some had been shot several times, and clumsily; the executioners either had poor aim or were interested in dealing out as much pain as they could before finishing the job.

The wall in back of Hahn was pockmarked by gunfire and spattered with patches of blood that had quickly dried to a dark brown under the afternoon sun.

Azhmeh now came to inspect the site of the massacre, and regarded the bodies without registering any emotion.

"Who were they?" Hahn asked tersely. "Why were they killed?"

Azhmeh shrugged. "People," he said. "They were just people. As to why they were killed, who knows? *In'shallah.*"

It might have been God's will, Hahn thought, but he suspected that the most likely culprit was not God, but someone who chose to appropriate His authority for himself.

There was another door at the other end of the courtyard, but by now Hahn had lost all enthusiasm for further exploration. With Azhmeh he returned to their previous place and remained there until it was time to move again.

Later, when the muezzin ascended to the top of his minaret and began to intone the evening prayers, Azhmeh decided that it was time to move in order to put the city behind them as soon as possible, no matter that the sun was still in the west. Ordinarily imperturbable, Azhmeh was suddenly restless, perhaps sensing dangers that Hahn was oblivious to.

Opening the door that led out onto the street, Azhmeh motioned Hahn forward. The street was empty, but this fact didn't reassure either of them. A man's crumpled body lay halfway up the block to their left; both of his hands, Hahn observed, were missing, but the blood that had flowed from the two stumps had dried long ago.

"A thief," Azhmeh said. "They do this to looters."

What form of mutilation, Hahn wondered, was reserved for spies?

They turned to the right, then started running. While the sun was closer to the horizon, the daytime heat had still not surrendered its hold on the city, and it was difficult to expend the energy necessary for swift movement. Hahn's throat was soon terribly parched and the warm water he sipped from his small canteen did little to relieve his thirst.

Now the street narrowed dramatically and veered sharply to the left as it descended into a welter of dark, ominous-looking passageways.

"Here we must be extra careful," Azhmeh advised.

Proceeding with agonizing slowness, he lifted the PK Walther out of his pocket, a signal to Hahn that he should do the same.

"You are sure this is the right direction?" asked the American.

He had long since lost all sense of where he was and felt that they had been moving in circles, traveling through the same streets over and over again.

"Of course. This is my neighborhood," Azhmeh replied.

The sound of gunfire subsided all at once, perhaps, Hahn speculated, because the antagonists were observing evening prayers. The muezzin's amplified voice could still be heard and only occasionally would his ululations be punctuated by a burst of an automatic.

Azhmeh stopped so suddenly that Hahn almost stumbled into him. "What is it?" he asked the Arab.

Azhmeh was listening for something. He made a gesture, indicating that Hahn should move back into the relative safety of a cobbler's doorway. Inside, the shop was dark and unoccupied, workbenches and tables had been thrown over, and tools and hundreds of shoes lay strewn over the floor.

Hahn heard the sudden wail of a child outside. Then he saw Azhmeh drop to one knee at the same time as the wall above Hahn's head disintegrated in a cloud of dust. Hahn threw himself to the ground, and in a moment, two men, their heads half-covered by white keffiyahs, appeared on the roof of a building across the way. They were brandishing Soviet-made AK-47's.

Azhmeh returned their fire, and the two heads disappeared from sight. A moment later answering gunfire came from the roof.

From their position, the Arabs could keep Azhmeh and Hahn pinned down indefinitely. But at the same time they had little chance of hitting either of them so long as they remained in the protection of the cobbler's shop.

"There will be more of them," Azhmeh. "We must do something now."

"What would you suggest? If we try to run now, we'll both be killed."

Azhmeh agreed, and proposed that they wait until it grew darker, when they might hope to escape.

"Maybe another hour," he assured Hahn, though without sounding optimistic himself.

Periodically over the next hours, the two gunmen would loose a barrage down onto the street in front of the cobbler's shop, tearing up much of the wall and shuttered doorway but otherwise inflicting no harm. It was simply their way of demonstrating that they were still there and would soon dispatch the infidels to another world.

It was Hahn's impression that, though they were probably working for the Mullah, these men were more or less operating on their own. If they had been in radio contact with a command post of some kind, then surely reinforcements would have already been summoned. It was even possible that this Kalashnikov-bearing pair had no loyalty to anyone, that they were simply indulging in their own, personally motivated butchery.

Not that their motives made any difference to Hahn. Whatever they were, if they shot you, you were dead.

Finally Azhmeh judged that the darkness was adequate to allow them to leave their position. "It is possible we will become separated," he warned. "If so, you follow this street all the way. It comes to the end of Medenine. Then you will see the road which you must take to meet your friends."

While the instructions didn't seem very complicated, Hahn suspected they wouldn't be easy to execute.

"I will go first," Azhmeh announced. "You wait and see what happens to me."

"I can try to distract them," Hahn suggested, showing him the .22. Azhmeh shrugged, not especially interested.

"Do as you wish," he said.

Without further word, Azhmeh got down on all fours

and began crawling, easing his body through the narrow gap created by the space between the half-lowered shutter and the threshold of the shop.

There hadn't been any fire from across the street in the last twenty minutes, but Hahn hardly expected that the gunmen had become bored and given up.

Hahn peered through the doorway just in time to see Azhmeh raise himself partway off the ground and break into a run. Predictably, the AK-47's opened up, dislodging fragments from the street behind Azhmeh.

Hahn squeezed himself under the shutter, deciding that it was senseless to delay, but before he could get to his feet, he heard a scream and looked up to see Azhmeh stagger and fall.

Disregarding his own safety for the moment, Hahn rushed to him, zigzagging to avoid the automatic fire and dropping abruptly when the bullets came too close. He clung to the cobbles, daring not to move. In the absence of light he hoped that the two gunmen would think he'd been struck. In fact, after a few desultory bursts from their machine guns, they ceased fire and approached the edge of their rooftop position. As they looked down into the street to see how successful they'd been, they began to talk excitedly. To Hahn they both sounded very young, like adolescents whose voices had just begun to change.

He was still a few yards from Azhmeh. At first he thought he was dead but then he saw his leg move. Azhmeh groaned and attempted to pull himself up into a sitting position, but this only succeeded in alerting the gunmen on the rooftop. They simultaneously opened up on him, practically tearing his body in two.

On the edge of panic, Hahn forced himself to remain motionless. Eventually, he reasoned, they would have to give him a moment to escape as they came down from the rooftop.

Finally one of the gunmen left the roof, leaving his companion to monitor the situation from above.

Hahn knew that the young gunman approaching him was about to give him the coup de grace. There was no chance he could escape his bullets if he continued to lie here.

But he didn't want to alert the gunman until the last possible moment, which meant that Hahn wasn't able to turn his head to see where he was. He had to rely on his hearing.

The gunman was making it easy for him, though, his footsteps, as he approached, sounding loud and confident against the ruptured stone pavement.

The gunman was only a few paces away. He had to move now, before he felt the press of the AK-47 against his head.

But nothing seemed real. While he had sometimes contemplated his own death, he had never imagined it would occur in an anonymous passageway in some obscure Tunisian city.

Afraid that he might be too paralyzed to act, he suddenly rolled to one side, firing before he really had an accurate view of his assailant. The sound of the bullets discharging seemed muffled to him, and for an instant he wondered if they'd had any effect whatsoever.

Then he saw the gunman tottering backward, the khaki color of his uniform suddenly turning bright red. There was an expression of vast surprise on his face, but no pain, and after a moment or two the young Arab lowered his eyes to survey the damage to his chest.

Again Hahn fired, his aim much better this time. A small hole opened up on one side of the gunman's cheek, duplicated almost immediately by a hole on the other side. It was by no means a critical wound, but it had a decisive impact, causing him to lose hold of his Kalashnikov and drop clumsily to the ground.

Wasting no more time, Hahn sprang up, instantly stumbling on a recent heap of camel dung and tumbling back down onto the pavement. As successive bursts of fire from the rooftop gunman tore through the air over his head, he silently expressed his thanks to the camel for saving his life.

In a second he got up again, veering to the left into the shelter of a stall sustaining damage from the AK-47 that was intended for him.

At this point he was far enough away to be out of the second gunman's range. Moreover, with the darkness and the sharp and repeated angles of the streets, there was little likelihood that the man would ever find him.

Although he fully anticipated more trouble in escaping through the precincts of Medenine, he didn't encounter any more gunmen. Much to his amazement, he was all at once on the fringes of the city, the paved streets and stone structures having given way to sand and clusters of mud-baked houses that appeared too flimsy to withstand the strong desert winds.

From this distance he could barely hear the whine of tracer bullets or the occasional detonating grenade. The mud-baked houses looked abandoned; there was no sign of life anywhere. However, Hahn did notice a flag flying from the top of a nearby water tower. He had never seen the design before—a crescent and a star in the middle of a violent red and green field. He guessed that it was meant to represent the newly unified state of Libya and Tunisia.

He continued walking until he came upon the main

highway. Astonished that Azhmeh's directions had been this easy to follow, he still had no assurance that he would be able to find Hunt and Shaw. The linkup was scheduled for ten-thirty p.m. at Km 40, but it was past nine now and he had yet to see a marker indicating where along the highway he was.

But he did get to his destination on time. A small blue marker, half-submerged in sand, confirmed that he was in the right place. His relief was short-lived, however, when he looked about him at the limitless horizon of sand and stunted palms. He appeared to be the only person left in the world, in this part of the world anyhow. With his water running out, he would soon have no choice but to return to Medenine and a fate he was certainly not looking forward to.

Ten minutes passed before Hahn detected the faint rumble of a chopper. He scanned the night sky, but he wasn't able to see it for another few minutes. When it did come into view, hovering darkly for an instant above the low-lying mountains before banking into its descent, Hahn noted that it was a Bell 214A, a more powerful version of the helicopters employed in the war in Vietnam.

Two men came out of the cloud of sand stirred up by the chopper's landing.

Hahn stayed where he was until the men identified themselves as Hunt and Shaw.

Hunt was the taller of the two, and Hahn thought he must be a Texan, although he couldn't say exactly why. Perhaps it was his lean frame, the guarded way he had of looking at people, and his rugged, tanned face. Otherwise the most remarkable thing about him was the black bushy eyebrows that all but dominated his face. Shaw, on the other hand, was the sort of person you could pick out as an asset from a thousand miles away. He had the body of a wrestler and the look of a pit bull. In the movies his type would be cast as a Mafia underling—dangerously erratic, maybe psychopathic.

"You De Stael?" Hunt called out over the sound of the helicopter.

"Affirmative."

"We have orders from Clausewitz to take you with us."

"Back to Tunis?"

"Other direction," Shaw said.

"Libya?"

"That's right."

"Clausewitz says that you're his eyes; he wants you to observe Undercross."

Undercross? Hahn at first didn't recall any such code name. Then it came back to him—an operation that was to entail thousands of men, an all-out assault against Qaddafi.

When he asked Shaw about it, he was surprised to learn that fewer than sixty men were involved. With a thousand he would have felt secure. With fifty-five he felt the opposite. Though he'd come through Medenine unscathed, he wasn't at all convinced that his luck would hold.

"Why does Clausewitz see a need for an observer? He has you," Hahn demanded as he followed them into the chopper.

"I have no idea. You'll have to ask him yourself," said Hunt. "Now strap yourself in."

He complied, and a moment later the chopper lifted off, stirring up clouds of sand. The star-lit desert fell away, and soon it was impossible to know whether the desolate-looking terrain below was Tunisia or Libya.

TELEPHONE CONVERSATION
TRANSCRIPT   JULY 28, 1986

Call initiated in Moscow
Logged in at 2:42 p.m., EDT.

Kadiyev: Mr. President, I am pleased to introduce myself. I am Alexei Kadiyev.

(Hereafter all remarks of Mr. Kadiyev are translated by the First Secretary's interpreter V. Shikanovich.)

President: I have long looked forward to talking to you, Mr. First Secretary. I hope that someday we shall have an opportunity to meet face-to-face.

(The President's remarks are translated by his interpreter, Bailey Myers.)

Kadiyev: I also will look forward to such a meeting. Please accept my apologies for the delay in returning your call. This shall not occur in the future. I understand that you have expressed to President Pomorov your concern over the movements of our fleet in the Mediterranean.

President: That is correct. The United States Government cannot separate the presence of your fleet in Libyan territorial waters from the alarming buildup of Libyan troops near Tunisia. As you must be aware, Libyan forces have

in fact crossed the border with Tunisia at
several points and are posing a threat to Tunisian sovereignty.

Kadiyev: I am aware of such reports, yes. But I
must stress to you, Mr. President, that the
Soviet Union and all peace-loving people have
no intention of provoking war with anyone.
But we have seen that the Sixth Fleet has taken
up a position that endangers the security of
Libya. We would like to have your guarantee
that Libyan integrity will not be jeopardized
and fervently protest these saber-rattling
maneuvers on your part.

President: I think we are talking at cross-pur-
poses here, Mr. Secretary. If anyone is doing
the saber-rattling it is your country. The world
already knows of your provocative actions in
Moroccan waters, and in addition, the United
States is in possession of intelligence indicating
that a missile installation in Libya, operated by
East Germans, was responsible for bringing
down one of our satellites on the 17th of July.
I have hesitated to make this public so as not
to escalate tension, but the absence of a retaliatory response—so far—should not be taken
as a sign of weakness, of restraint. Any further
incident of this kind will invite a prompt and
powerful response.

Kadiyev: May I suggest that your failure to respond already was not due to your fears of
provoking war, but rather to your recognition
that these allegations are baseless? Neither the

Soviet Union nor any of her allies has perpetrated such attacks as you describe. If one of your satellites failed, then perhaps the cause lies in your faulty technology. But let me state categorically, Mr. President, that we are as interested in maintaining the peace as you declare yourselves to be. I can assure you that if the United States makes no effort to undermine the security of Libya then you have nothing to fear from us.

President: You are not addressing the problem the Libyans are posing to Tunisia.

Kadiyev: I know only that certain factions within Tunisia have been demonstrating against the regime and that there have been repeated calls for a merger with Libya by patriotic Tunisians. Most assuredly, the Soviet Union will not act to stop a merger that is in the interests of the two peoples if that is their wish.

President: We have reason to believe that it is not their wish and will take whatever steps necessary to prevent a forcible merger from taking place.

Kadiyev: I again say to you, Mr. President, that in the event of a violation of Libyan security the Soviet Union will have no choice but to act. I wish you a very good day.

Conversation terminates at 2:55 p.m., EDT.

17

By three in the afternoon the mosque was practically devoid of worshippers. It was small, out-of-the-way, and in desperate need of repair. The sunlight filtering down from the dome illuminated the dusty interior.

From time to time the silence inside the mosque would be shattered by the distant rattle of gunfire or the piercing wail of a police siren. But such sounds had become so usual that the few old men praying there paid them no heed. They might also simply have been hard of hearing.

The arrival of another worshipper, wrapped in a white djbella, went ignored. Carefully, he removed his shoes and proceeded into the mosque, where he took up a reverential posture by the side of a lone figure squatted in the corner.

In a whisper the new arrival said, "I bring greetings from Azer."

The man responded to the prearranged signal exactly as he was supposed to: "You may tell Azer that he is always welcome in the house of my people." He looked at the new arrival, who had pushed his djbella partway off his face, revealing his features. Lisker smiled. It was Kolnikov.

Lisker, the earlier arrival at the mosque, had laid eyes on Kolnikov only once before, in the Agadir hotel lobby, and it should have fallen to Zoccola to consummate any deal with the Russian. But Kolnikov had surprised them and left Morocco on orders from his superiors. The upheaval in Tunisia required that he report on the radicals' progress in ousting the pro-Western regime and that he liaise with the new Libyan-backed government that was expected to replace it.

As Drexell preferred keeping Zoccola in Fez to attend the Third World conference, Lisker had been assigned the task of concluding negotiations with Mr. Clean. While Drexell had not given his reasons, Lisker suspected that he was chosen because of his military background. Of all the members of Triad he was best equipped to assess the deteriorating situation in Tunis and very likely the best equipped to escape from it.

So far the worst aspect of this mission was having to wear this outlandish disguise, one which appeared to amuse Kolnikov though, in truth, the Russian looked no less absurd wrapped in his own djbella.

"I am pleased that you responded so quickly to my message," Kolnikov said in a hushed voice.

"Events demand haste."

"Indeed. I understand that you lost my previous gift to you. You should not have been so careless."

"There was a leak to your people somewhere,"

"You are not blaming me, are you?" Kolnikov blustered quietly, his djbella shaking with indignation.

"If we did I wouldn't be here," he replied tersely. In contrast to Zoccola who tended to enjoy a little banter in his transactions, Lisker was all business.

"Yes, I see that. You are authorized to offer me what I wish."

"If your demands don't turn out to be excessive."

"First off, I want you to know that whatever amount of money you can provide is not likely to be enough."

Lisker wasn't prepared for this. Was it just a maneuver, an extreme opening position in a protracted negotiation?

But Kolnikov was dead serious. He *was* interested in something more elaborate—and more profitable—than a simple payoff.

"In Moscow," he said, "I have access to jewelry, to gold, to foreign currency. If I am to work regularly for you, I need to have markets available for these things in the West."

As troubled as Lisker was by the Russian's demands, he knew Drexell thought Kolnikov important enough that they should go to some lengths to accommodate him. As a high-ranking officer in the defense intelligence, he might provide them with information of the greatest value regarding Soviet intentions in the region.

But it was one thing to try and arrange a conduit for channeling information and money back and forth, and altogether another to organize a large-scale smuggling operation.

"I think we'd be willing to find a solution," Lisker said, his expression taut, "but I'll need some time to see whether we can work it out."

"There is no time available. The information I will give you will be at my disposal only today. If you fail to exploit this opportunity it will be gone forever."

In a final attempt to delay making a commitment to the elaborate smuggling scheme, Lisker tried to convince the Russian that he was already taking such a grave risk passing military secrets to the Americans that he would only place himself in still greater jeopardy by becoming involved in major smuggling. He reminded him of the fate that Boris the Gypsy had suffered five years before. One of Russia's top circus officials, Boris was arrested when he was found to be concealing in excess of one million rubles worth of diamonds and foreign currency in his apartment.

"I am more clever than Boris the Gypsy," Kolnikov said when Lisker had finished. Then with his characteristic fatalism he added, "If I am caught, so I am caught." He did not, however, sound as though he expected this would happen any time soon.

Lisker was grimly silent, then he finally committed himself—and by extension the Task Force and the President of the United States. "We will make the necessary guarantees."

"Excellent," said Kolnikov as he got up off his knees. "Someone will be in touch with you tonight. He will instruct you on how to pick up the information. At the same time, you will receive the specifications for payments to me and for the drops here and in Morocco. Good day."

Lisker waited several minutes before following the Russian out of the mosque.

To get back to where he was staying, Lisker relied on public buses and the power of his own two feet. As anti-American sentiment was rife, he kept his disguise. Wherever Lisker went, the walls were strewn with slogans in English, French, and Arabic calling for revolution while advocating death for "satanists" and "imperialists," two categories into which Americans, innocent or not, apparently fell. Shooting could be heard with ever greater frequency, though it was impossible to say who was shooting at whom.

Nonetheless, it was clear that whole sections of the city—particularly the native quarter—were no longer under the effective control of Tunisian authorities in spite of the display of tanks and soldiers on the main boulevards and in the public squares.

The first few contingents of troops sent by the French were visible in the streets close to the administrative district; they were Legionnaires—the 1st Regiment Etranger de Gavalerie, which was a part of the intervention force GUEPARD, ordinarily stationed in Orange, France. Their motto was Nec Pluribus Impart—Unequal to None.

These Legionnaires, hard and war-seasoned, stood in knots in front of their light-armored cars (Panhard AML's), which bore 9mm MAT-49 submachine guns. They made for an intimidating show of force, but in the event of a general uprising Lisker doubted that they could do more than fight a rearguard action.

Other French contingents—the 1st Regiment Étranger airlifted last night from Aubagne, France; two companies of the Groupement Operationnel de Legion Etranger (GOLE) brought in from their base in Corsica; and a unit of the Force de Frappe transferred from the Central African Republic—had been recently sent to the disputed border area to supplement the Tunisian army.

In manpower the Tunisian army could hardly be considered well-endowed; it had approximately 25,000 men—compared to double that number for Libya. The Tunisians were equipped with seventy-five tanks, only a few of which represented advanced technology. Libya, by contrast, had about 3,000 tanks, the majority new and recently furnished by the Soviet Union. In terms of combat aircraft Tunisia had perhaps a dozen, the Libyans close to 500 supplemented by forty armed helicopters. The Tunisians had no missiles for their air-force, while the Libyans could rely on air-to-air, air-to-surface, and surface-to-air missiles.

It was unlikely that the addition of French forces, no matter how efficient, could alter the odds against the Tunisians.

The situation prevailing in the capital had changed so dramatically in the last several days that, before his arrival, Lisker had decided to forgo a luxury room at the Hilton in favor of an obscure, rather derelict, hotel on the fringes of the city. In further hopes of avoiding attention, he decided not to remain at this place for more than a day or two.

When he returned to his room on the fifth floor, a room which gave him a view of a retaining wall of stucco and nothing else, he discovered that he had a visitor. It was Sayid al-Gazzar, the Tunisian chief of security. With him were three heavily armed escorts who had taken up position outside the door. If Lisker had hoped for anonymity he was obviously disappointed. After tonight, he would have to move.

The two men had never encountered each other before but Lisker recognized the official from photographs. In person he looked shorter, less the burly, commanding presence who had kept the country safe for the Bourguibas than a tired man who could have been a professor of history at an undistinguished university.

Whether Drexell had provided him with the information necessary to find him or whether al-Gazzar had done so on his own Lisker was unable to find out. "That is unimportant," the security chief cut off Lisker brusquely.

Seating himself on his mattress, Lisker waited to see what al-Gazzar wanted from him.

It wasn't what he had expected.

"I wish you to arrange with your superiors to provide

me and my family with sanctuary in your country.''

"You can't give up hope yet," Lisker responded, at the same time hiding his incredulity.

If the head of security was seeking sanctuary in America, then it was obvious that the situation in Tunisia had deteriorated more markedly than they had all suspected.

"I am very serious, Mr. Lisker. I am on the fanatics' death list, there is no question. Tonight, in order to keep up appearances, I leave to go to Fez with Premier Kalek as part of the delegation. But I will not be returning here. I would like to have assurances that there will be a place for me in the United States. I need protection. In Morocco, even in France, the situation for me is very dangerous. And if Tunisia goes, Morocco will be next. So you see my dilemma?''

"I am to assume then that you expect a Libyan takeover?''

"The Libyans will not advance or they will, it does not matter. But the Islamic fanatics, they have taken control of the populace. I try to be a realist, Mr. Lisker. I know what happened to the Shah. The Bourguibas are making preparations to go into exile at this very moment.''

Lisker had a vision of thousands of government officials pounding desperately on the doors of the American embassy. "Have you been in touch with the U.S. Ambassador?" Lisker asked.

"I do not trust the ambassador. It is my belief that you are in a more reliable position to assist me.''

Lisker didn't respond to the implication of the statement. He explained, "The people I work with aren't here in Tunis. I'll speak with them today and then have someone get in contact with you in Fez.''

Al-Gazzar regarded him dubiously. Under other cir-

cumstances he might have threatened Lisker with retaliatory action if his request was not met. Instead he
said only, ''Remember that I am still in charge of the
security of American personnel in this country,'' but his
declaration was meaningless. Aside from a skeletal staff
remaining on in the embassy, most American nationals
had departed from Tunisia the previous week. The
threat was especially absurd since al-Gazzar was just
hours away from abandoning ship himself. He had only
limited jurisdiction left; probably three-quarters of the
country had slipped out of his hands in the last seventy-
two hours.

The two men shook hands stiffly, then al-Gazzar
turned and left the room.

Lisker wasn't concerned about al-Gazzar's fate; that
would be up to Drexell to decide. But there could now
be little doubt as to the fate of Tunisia. That was something that not even Drexell could do very much about.

18

William Drexell had moved into the Banc Union-Reserve. While the bank did provide financial services for the local population as well as for an international clientele, it had actually been established jointly by American and French intelligence services to funnel information in and out of North Africa. The same communications apparatus used for transferring funds from Tangier to the Grand Cayman Island or New York was also used for relaying secret data back to the White House and the Élysée Palace.

The communications room on the top floor of the Banc Union-Reserve provided an unsurpassed panorama of the ancient capital: a honeycomb of stucco houses and domed mosques punctuated by soaring minarets.

On a clear day—as this was—it was also possible to make out the roof of the National Handicrafts Center where the Third World conference was now under way.

Below the impressive panorama of the ancient capital, Drexell faced a bank of computer terminals which, much to his surprise, functioned perfectly despite the occasional unreliability of the local power company.

Even in his light-weight khaki jacket and matching slacks, which looked like the outfit of someone trekking across the Sahara, Drexell still radiated a commanding presence. Though many of those in the room had no idea what role he played in the operations, they instinctively turned to him for instructions.

The fact was, though, that Drexell himself felt somewhat out of place among all these terminals and advanced communications equipment. Accustomed to the demands of real combat, he couldn't quite make the adjustment to contending with war and revolution at one remove. A computer screen filling up with statistics, maps, projections, and a continuous barrage of situation reports did not, to his mind, make it easier to cope with events. He supposed, though, that he'd one day have to get used to these gadgets, for future wars would no doubt be fought and won—or lost—at consoles like these.

A steady stream of information continued to pour in around the clock from Washington, Paris, the communication command of the Sixth Fleet, reconnaissance satellites, and, occasionally, from the streets directly outside the walls of this makeshift situation room.

The night before, in Fez and in virtually all the major cities in Morocco—Casablanca, Rabat, Agadir, Tangier, and Marrakesh—leaflets had been clandestinely distributed by opponents of King Hassan's regime. The leaflets, one of which was now in Drexell's hands, all bore the same message:

THE TYRANT HASSAN IS PREPARING TO RAISE THE PRICES OF BREAD, SUGAR,

GRAIN, COTTON, BEEF, LAMB, COFFEE, AND TEA! THESE PRICES WILL DOUBLE AND TRIPLE! THE PEOPLE OF MOROCCO WILL STARVE WHILE THE IMPERIALISTS ENGORGE THEMSELVES! DEMONSTRATE! TAKE TO THE STREETS! BRING DOWN THE OPPRESSORS!

The leaflet was signed by the People's Redemption Committee.

"No one's ever heard of this organization," commented Cavanaugh, who had spoken half an hour before with the chief of police in Fez. "It might be the Communists, the fundamentalists, or an alliance of various dissident forces. But whoever put them out had their act together. They've cropped up everywhere at the same time, and it's all the police can do to take them down."

"Any reactions to them?" Drexell's hard expression was the only sign of the strain he had been under these last several days, as North Africa veered more and more out of control.

"We have reports of scattered outbreaks of violence, but they seem to be confined to cities in the south and west. The government keeps issuing denials over national radio. Hassan especially doesn't want to be embarrassed at a time he's gathering together so many heads of state. But the thing the authorities fear most is a run on the shops, the development of a hoarding situation."

Since there seemed little that Drexell could do regarding that particular problem, he turned back to his main concerns—Tunisia and the south of Morocco.

The information that Mr. Clean had supplied to Lisker in Tunis had reached his desk only that morning, conveyed by diplomatic pouch to the American consul in Fez.

If it was accurate, and Drexell had little cause to think that it was not, the Soviets had made a decision to intervene only should events go so much against Qaddafi that his regime was seriously threatened. Otherwise their presence in the Gulf of Sidra and fifteen miles off the coast of Tunisia—three miles beyond the territorial limit —was intended only as a show of force. But whether this meant that they would restrain themselves if American forces became directly involved in shoring up the tottering government of Tunisia was a question that Kolnikov's documentation did not answer.

Moreover, from what Lisker had reported it seemed that anything short of sending in U.S. troops would fail to save the country from going under. Riots were continuing to erupt throughout Tunisia and it was widely expected that the government of Prime Minister Kalek would fall in twenty-four to forty-eight hours.

More promising was the information Kolnikov had provided on the situation in south Morocco. Here, perhaps, something could be done. The renewed campaign by Polisario insurgents was obviously being coordinated with the activation of the Libyan armed forces, but it was unclear as to how prepared the Polisario was to undertake a campaign which was to strike simultaneously at Moroccan defenses in the "Triangle"—an area in the contested Western Sahara rich in phosphorus and fortified by mines and electric fences—and at cities and army installations within Morocco itself. To Drexell it appeared unlikely that the insurgents could maintain a war effort of such magnitude for long without dangerously stretching their supply and communication lines. Never before had the Polisario attempted such an all-out assault. Either they were overconfident or else were

confident of success for some real, but as yet undi-
vulged, reason. Drexell suspected the latter.

"According to the information from Kolnikov, the
Polisario campaign is to begin tomorrow," Drexell told
Cavanaugh, "timed to coincide with the opening of the
Third World conference. I have no doubt that it's being
coordinated by the Soviets to divert attention from
what's happening in Libya and Tunisia," he concluded,
instructing Cavanaugh to personally present the Polisario battle plan to the relevant Moroccan authorities.
Conveniently, the latter were all within half a dozen
blocks of the King, who was staying at a villa put at his
majesty's disposal until he returned to his home palace
in Rabat.

"You might also convey my regrets to Mr. Diab that
I won't be able to make the reception he's throwing
for Kalek tonight," Drexell added. "I'm sure I'll be
missed."

"I have a feeling you might have engineered this
whole crisis to give yourself an excuse to stay away,"
Cavanaugh suggested mildly.

Drexell almost smiled.

One of the lines in front of him hooked Drexell directly in to the White House; the communication was
established via satellite, avoiding entirely the uncertain
Moroccan telecommunications system.

The President was not immediately available, Drexell
was informed by a White House aide—he was in the
middle of an address to representatives of the construc-
tion industry at Washington's Shoreham Hotel, but he
would get back to Drexell as soon as possible.

Cursing the President, as well as the beleaguered con-
struction industry, Drexell next tried to contact Hahn,
who should now be with Undercross somewhere in the

Libyan province of Tripolitania. Having crossed into Libya thirty-six hours previously, the force should have been small and mobile enough to elude frontier patrols and penetrate into the Libyan countryside undetected.

In the temporary absence of Cavanaugh, Drexell established the shortwave transmission himself. "This is Clausewitz calling Charlie. Do you read me, Charlie? Over."

Several moments later, through a thick cloud of static, he was rewarded with a response.

"This is Charlie, Clausewitz. Go ahead. We read you."

From the Texas accent he could tell it was Hunt, not Hahn. No matter. He would talk to Hahn later on. "Advise for status, Charlie. Over."

"We're at coordinates two-zero-zero-alpha, four-one-four-one-romeo. Over."

"That's two-zero-zero-alpha, four-one-four-one-romeo."

Checking his own map, Drexell noted that commando group Charlie was exactly where it should be, north of Al Hamrah desert approximately one hundred miles from the Tunisian border. "Any problems on your end? Over."

"Everything is proceeding smoothly. No evidence of opposition here, just lots of desert. Over."

The transmission had to be kept short in order to avoid having their location revealed by triangulation.

"Excellent. I'll be back to you on our alternate frequency at 21:22 hours for a final determination. If there's a problem keep tuned in until 23:30 hours. If you don't hear by then we'll have to scratch it. Over."

"Understood. We will be waiting. Over and out."

For the first time that day there seemed nothing for

Drexell to do but wait. As much as he needed to be in control, he had, for the moment, exhausted his options.

Having had almost no sleep the previous few nights, he decided to close his eyes for just a few minutes.

He was out like a light in his chair for the next three hours and would have remained that way but for the sudden ringing of the telephone.

TELEPHONE CONVERSATION
TRANSCRIPT   JULY 30

Telephone call initiated by the White House
Logged at 10:05 a.m., EDT.

President: Bill, how are you holding up?

Drexell: I'm waiting for an update on Under-
            cross.

President: You'll let me know as soon as you hear
            anything?

Drexell: Of course.

President: I just spent most of the night with
            Marty and we've decided we have no choice
            but to respond to the Libyans. I'm sending the
            Nimitz and some support ships right into the
            Gulf of Sidra.

Drexell: We've done that before.

President: This time, though, I'm going to order
            our aircraft to undertake reconnaissance

flights over strategic Libyan positions in Libya and Tunisia.

Drexell: That'll prove interesting.

President: If the Libyans attack, we will meet it with an appropriate response.

Drexell: If you don't mind my saying so, it seems that you've had quite a change of heart since our last conversation.

President: Before this, I really didn't have any idea how bad the situation was over there. I'm not sure we can do anything to keep Tunisia from going under, but I want it made clear to that bastard in Tripoli we're not about to take this lying down. Keep me posted, Bill.

Conversation terminates at 10:10 a.m., EDT.

19

Hahn recognized the trucks, he recognized their make, and he knew their history. There were as many as twenty-five of them strung out along the road. They were all identical heavy-duty trucks, manufactured in the United States in 1978 by the Oshkosh Truck Corporation of Wisconsin and sold to Libya with the proviso that they would only be employed for agricultural purposes. All 400 trucks ordered by the Libyans had been converted, in flagrant violation of this proviso, to military transport capable of hauling Soviet-made tanks. Though it was past twilight Hahn could, with the pair of Nikon binoculars lent him, make out the type of tanks riding on the Oshkosh trucks. Several were older models of the SP type, but most were ZSU-23-4's, often used in action in this part of the world, each with four 23mm AA cannons that could get off 1000 rounds each. Finally, there was a gun dish radar mounted on a PT-76 tank chassis.

Hahn wouldn't have been surprised if this was some

of the same military equipment first captured on film by cameras on board the U.S. spy satellite weeks before.

Shaw, Hunt, and Hahn were observing the passage of the trucks through the vast wasteland from the concealment of a dry stream bed called a wadi.

"Be nice if we could take them out," Shaw said.

Hahn had the impression that the menacing-looking man wouldn't have minded taking anyone out—just for a change of pace.

"We did that in Rhodesia, you remember?" Hunt put in. "We were facing an advance patrol of Mugabe's troops, threw ourselves right at them, blew the shit out of them."

Shaw evidently had been in on the same operation.

"Christ," he said, "you should've seen the looks in their eyes when they ran out of the brush—and boom! That was some kind of good time."

"Mugabe still won," Hahn couldn't help noting.

Hunt glowered. Shaw merely shrugged.

Realizing too late that this remark would only alienate them from him more than they already were, he decided to play safe and return to the subject at hand.

"Hell, if we didn't have to worry about alerting the Libyans to our presence here, we could demolish the convoy, no problem," Hahn said enthusiastically.

"No problem," Hunt repeated sarcastically. "Ain't life a bitch?"

"It's full of frustrations," Shaw agreed.

The last day and a half had been the same thing. Trusting neither Shaw nor Hunt, and unable to communicate with the Libyan mercenaries who spoke mostly Arabic and, in any case, regarded the Americans with a wariness that bordered on suspicion, Hahn had learned to stay mainly to himself. Seeing how mindless the advisers as well as the mercenaries were, Hahn began to understand why Drexell needed him as his eyes and ears on this operation; there was no one else he could really rely on.

Once the caravan of trucks had receded and the rumble of their motors was no longer audible, the commandos resumed their journey.

They were riding in all-terrain vehicles to reach their destination—the site of the Orbital Transport and Raketen Aktiengesellschaft—but there would be Bell helicopters available to take them out of the country once the operation was completed.

A brief sandstorm soon turned the sky into the color of jaundice, blotting out all visibility and putting a temporary halt to their progress. The only positive aspect of the storm was that it covered over their tracks, making it that much harder for Libyan patrols to detect them.

"It's still possible Clausewitz will cancel," Shaw remarked after the sandstorm had subsided and they continued again.

"I'm pretty sure it'll be a go-ahead," Hahn replied.

He wondered if either Shaw or Hunt knew who Clausewitz was and decided that it was quite likely they didn't. They only knew that he was very high up, and that was all they needed to know.

"On an operation like this we don't ever see the big picture," Shaw said resentfully, implying that Hahn was better acquainted with the details of their mission than he and Hunt were.

"We'll know shortly one way or another," Shaw said, peering through the windshield at what resembled a tidal wave of sand created by the wind. "When is Clausewitz supposed to contact us?"

"Twenty-one hours twenty-two minutes," replied the Texan. "Twenty-three thirty at the latest."

"You think he'll be on time?" asked Shaw.

Hahn said that he was sure he would be.

Shaw was shaking his head. "Hell, nothing's on time in this part of the world. I've been around enough to know that much. You wait and see."

Early in the evening they drew up into the sanctuary of another wadi and settled in to wait for the radio communication.

Although they were in position, at a point approximately sixteen miles due east of ORTAG's location, they would have to be assured of aerial backup in order to go forward with the mission.

Twenty-one hundred hours passed. Then twenty-two hundred hours, and the radio remained silent. Shaw gave Hahn a knowing look. Hunt couldn't sit still; he was pacing back and forth, impatient for action.

At 22:38 the two-way radio came alive. "This is Clausewitz," Drexell's voice crackled through the night. "This is Clausewitz calling Charlie. Over."

"This is Charlie, Clausewitz. We read you," Shaw said. "Over."

"Is De Stael there?"

Shaw handed the transmitter to Hunt.

"This is De Stael. Over."

"Everything set? Over."

"We're ready. Over."

"The show is taking to the road. Duckblind at Sunrise. Do you read me? Over."

Duckblind at Sunrise indicated a go-ahead.

"We read you. Confirm Duckblind at Sunrise."

"Good luck to you then. Over and out."

"It's a go," Hahn said.

At that moment he didn't know whether to be exhilarated or scared shitless. He decided he was both.

Shaw quickly passed the word around and within ten minutes the commandos were fully mobilized. They

were now about to make their way to the assembly point
five miles northwest of the ORTAG installation.

Hahn had no idea of what to expect, and when they
arrived, he was surprised by how large it was. Set down
in the middle of the desert in a valley formed by three
mountains, the complex was surrounded first by barbed
wire, and then by high, electronically guarded steel
fences broken at intervals by watchtowers. Even in the
midnight gloom, it was possible for Hahn and Shaw,
situated on one of the mountain peaks, to make out the
turretlike silhouettes of the rockets, as well as the
honeycomb of houses, with their flat corrugated roofs,
where the technicians and manual workers apparently
lived. Although they were in possession of some of the
plans for the ORTAG base, the operations team still
could not have anticipated the size and scale of the
defense system.

"It's going to be harder than I thought," Shaw remarked tonelessly.

"But it has to be done before dawn," Hahn insisted.
"Once it's light we lose the element of surprise."

Shaw acknowledged Hahn's point. "We'll just have
to knock out what we can, cripple their launching
capacity, and get the hell out quick."

The six men with Hahn and Shaw constituted one of
the three reconnaissance patrols scouting the terrain.
They were not, however, the only patrols in the area.

It was on their way back to the assembly point, riding
in their Jeep, with its 105mm recoilless rifle mounted on
the rear, that Shaw caught sight of another vehicle
lumbering across the rock-strewn terrain, its lights cutting a swath along the ground ahead of it.

"Look over there," Shaw bellowed to Hahn.

Hahn looked and was afraid of what he saw.

It was a truck, a Soviet-made ZIL. There was no

question that its occupants were a part of a patrol. The ZIL was approaching them quickly, leaving little doubt that they'd been spotted.

The Jeep's driver, a youthful Libyan, slewed their vehicle sharply to the right, almost directly into the path of the oncoming truck.

"What the hell's he doing?" Hahn shouted. He would have thought it made more sense to go in the opposite direction.

No one could answer. "Get the fuck down," Shaw said and then, without waiting for a response, pushed Hahn brutally down into the Jeep.

The Jeep right behind theirs had also come to a halt, sliding into the sand from the abrupt application of its brakes.

Shaw was shouting to the other vehicle through his two-way radio. "Fire at the goddamn son of a bitch. Fire."

Someone began firing from the vehicle behind them as their Libyan driver scrambled to the rear of the Jeep to take hold of the recoilless rifle mounted there.

Before he could get off a single round, Hahn heard him scream. Oblivious to the danger, he lifted his head and saw the man clasp his hands to his chest and pitch over onto the sand.

"Aw fuck," Shaw said, more out of annoyance than fear. He moved toward the back of the Jeep himself.

Hahn felt strangely abandoned. Nonetheless, he got out his .32 and held it, waiting for the proper moment to use it.

Shaw stayed low, crawling back toward the gun mount. The recoilless rifle on the other Jeep was now spitting a stream of bullets in the direction of the ZIL. The tracers formed streaks of bright blue in the darkness.

Seizing the gun, Shaw sighted it on the ZIL's chassis as bullets from the Russian truck whipped over his head.

As Hahn watched, Shaw's action paid off as the ZIL took several hits in its gas tank and motor. Smoke erupted from out of the hood. A moment later, half the truck seemed to come apart with an enormous roar and a spurt of blue and crimson flames.

After the ZIL settled to earth again, four or five men leaped from its charred ruins. They weren't Libyans, but Germans—East Germans.

One man was covered with flames. He threw himself on the ground and rolled over and over in an effort to extinguish them, but to no avail. The flames appeared to peel away his face, and before long he was a shriveled, unidentifiable form lying in the waste.

Neither Shaw nor his comrade-in-arms firing the 105mm gun on the back of the other Jeep was prepared to offer mercy. They continued to lay down a withering barrage on the survivors.

Hahn aimed his gun but didn't fire. He watched as a man had his legs shot out from under him and flopped down into the sand. Shaw had been watching the man too, for he immediately turned his gun on him, drilling him full of bullets as he sprawled helplessly on the sand.

Hahn knew he should have been appalled at this savagery, but somehow he wasn't. An obscene sense of excitement had taken hold of him, and it was only heightened by the danger.

One of the Germans had managed to escape the commandos' gunfire and was now attempting to make his way down into a ravine in a steep descent that would prove difficult for the Jeeps to follow.

Without thinking, Hahn jumped from the Jeep and began racing after him.

It was hard to run in the sand with any speed, and when he reached the crest of the hill and looked down he could barely discern the fleeing soldier.

He was half-inclined to give up. One East German more or less wouldn't make much difference. And they had to assume that their intrusion had already been noted.

Nonetheless, he continued to pursue the soldier. Slipping in the dark as he ran, little by little, he began to bridge the distance between him and his prey.

The German heard him, turned and fired a burst from his AK-47, but the rounds landed harmlessly against the slope. Hahn returned the fire, and also failed to hit his target.

Then the German stumbled and fell, his weapon flying from his hand.

Before he could get back on his feet, Hahn was looming over him, his .32 pressed to the German's temple. It was a shock for Hahn to get a good look at him, to see how young he was, no more than twenty.

Hahn could understand a little German, but not enough to grasp what he was trying to tell him. Not that it mattered; the panic in the German's eyes was eloquent enough.

Hahn hesitated, then lowered his gun. He retrieved the Kalashnikov and motioned with it for the soldier to get up. They both started back up the hill, the German in front of him.

Hahn was halfway up when some rocks slid out from under him. He gashed his ankle and as he grabbed it in pain, the German began to make a run for it down the hill.

Hahn brought him down with one shot. The man simply cried out and collapsed. A few moments later, he managed to raise himself up and lurched ahead for a few paces before keeling over again. This time he stayed down.

Hahn stood staring at the lifeless figure, and would have remained there for some time if Shaw hadn't called down to him. "We're moving out," he warned.

Hahn went to rejoin the others.

By the time Hahn arrived at the Jeep, Shaw was already radioing instructions to Hunt, who'd stayed behind at the assembly point.

"Get those choppers into the air," Shaw was shouting, "prepare for drop over target area. And as soon as the decoy team is ready send them in."

Before they had returned to the assembly point, three of the five available choppers were in the sky, coasting over the mountains, then suddenly sweeping sharply down over the defense perimeters until they were positioned directly above the heart of the installation where the Atlas-Centaur and Delta rockets waited at their launching pads.

Although the assembly point was out of range of the base, those in the reserve units remaining there had only to look up at the sky to see evidence of the slowly developing conflict. Harsh green and yellow lights flashed repeatedly along the horizon as they heard the clatter of small arms fire and, periodically, loud detonations as salvos of rockets—guided Vaught-Lance battlefield-support weapons—were fired from the commandos' mobile launchers stationed beyond the outer perimeter onto the base.

From time to time the helicopter invaders would initiate radio contact with the command station. The first report was favorable: "Decoy team in, meeting little resistance here."

The second report was less so: "Chopper Charlie Alpha taken out, two pilots lost. All the others on the ground at Point Victor Beta Rome.''

''I guess we'll have to send another chopper to fish them out of there,'' was Shaw's only comment.

The explosions were increasing in frequency, the sky was turning as bright as high noon, and in the weird hazy light that the battle was casting up, Hahn could see the Bell helicopters seeming to float soundlessly in the air as, little by little, they descended to pull out members of the forward operations team.

Unable to contain his curiosity, Hahn commandeered one of the unused Jeeps, and drove to the summit of the nearest mountain so he could survey the scene for himself.

Unfortunately, about all that he could see was a thick cloud of blackish smoke that hung over the entirety of the base. Every so often one of the helicopters would dip down and vanish into the smoke only to reappear moments later. He couldn't account for these maneuverings.

While the glare of lights produced by the successive explosions was far more pronounced from this position, Hahn was still unable to determine how the battle was progressing or what kind of damage was being wrought. As he well knew, it was possible to set a great deal of equipment on fire and riddle it full of holes without succeeding in destroying its military capability.

But then he witnessed an astonishing spectacle; first one Delta rocket, then a second and a third, rose out of the smoke. As they gradually ascended into the sky, he saw that each's programmed trajectory set it off in a competely different direction. Yet they didn't get very far. Almost simultaneously each burst into flame and exploded, leaving swelling trails of smoke to trace their abrupt plunges back to earth.

Yet another rocket, this one much larger than the

Delta, burst through the layer of smoke and proceeded on a southwesterly bearing before it too disintegrated with an enormous din, and came plummeting straight back down.

It was suddenly clear to Hahn that the invaders had managed to seize the main launching station and were sending the rockets up in order to self-destruct them in the air. It was a considerably less time-consuming method of destruction than attempting to sabotage them on the ground.

No further rockets were launched, however, either because the station had been retaken or else because the forward team had achieved all it could.

The latter possibility seemed the more likely. As Hahn watched, two helicopters materialized from the whorls of smoke at the center of the base and began heading in his direction at the assembly point.

It looked to Hahn as if it might finally be time to go home.

20

Squadrons of heavily armed police and units drawn from the Moroccan army had been deployed in front of the National Handicrafts complex since the early-morning hours. But their presence didn't necessarily reassure Zoccola; the sheer number of delegates filing into the complex and the press of onlookers and demonstrators parading just beyond the wooden barriers had the authorities taxed to the limit. As limousine after limousine continued to roll up and disgorge its distinguished occupants, many in traditional national dress, it was all the police could do simply to corroborate the credentials presented to them. After a while, to smooth the admission process two additional doors to the complex were opened up.

Zoccola had been accorded observer status. He was the only representative from the Task Force available to attend the inaugural session of the Third World conference which King Hassan himself was to open. He hoped they wouldn't have to wait too long for things to get under way as the King was notorious for lateness.

The press area to which Zoccola was directed was a spacious glass-enclosed structure that overlooked a stage colorfully festooned with the flags of the invited nations. Each desk in the press area was provided with a set of earphones and a dialing mechanism that allowed the journalist to listen to the proceedings in whatever language he or she was familiar with.

Zoccola watched as security men with dogs trained to sniff explosives made a last-minute check of the stage, paying particular attention to the lectern and the throne, which was upholstered in crimson and adorned with the insignia of the Moroccan royal household.

Around him various journalists, from Guinea-Bissau and Australia, from Colombia and Canada, from Greece and Togoland, took their designated seats. They had the look of people who expected to rush off to their typewriters and teletype machines at any moment. But it wasn't King Hassan they were waiting to hear; it was Tunisia's Prime Minister Kalek. With the official government broadcasts out of Tunis so terse and uninformative, the question in the hall was whether Kalek would at last acknowledge publicly that his government had fallen.

Precisely at ten o'clock and heralded by a sudden rise in the volume of voices and a pronounced rustling of paper, the procession of presidents, prime ministers, foreign ministers, and titular heads of state began. As they marched in their slow, somewhat desultory, manner down the center aisle to the stage, a generous infusion of security people swelled their ranks, and took places beside the gradually seated dignitaries.

When they had all assembled, a military band sheltered in a cavity directly below the stage struck up a

spirited version of the Moroccan national anthem, and
the delegates stood.

Representatives of the Moroccan press also stood; the
others in the observation area remained seated, scrawl-
ing notes or adjusting their earphones to obtain a voice
speaking in a language they could understand.

Prime Minister Kalek was flanked on one side by his
Moroccan counterpart, Prime Minister Diab, and on
the other by the Tunisian security chief, Sayid al-
Gazzar, who looked rather abstracted. Several seats
away from Kalek, Zoccola noted another familiar face:
Indonesian Foreign Minister Adam Meureudu. After
the rousing finish of the anthem, Zoccola glanced
around and noticed that Adrienne Calenda had just
joined the press near the back of the room. Her eyes
seemed to be concentrated on her husband—though
without warmth—and so she didn't see Zoccola.
Though she might not remember him from their brief
encounter in Rabat, Zoccola moved to the vacant desk
next to hers.

She was wearing, he saw, a fashionable if somewhat
severe suit of tan. With her hair drawn back, she seemed
both resolute and unapproachable.

Despite the rather cold reception he expected from
her, he managed to catch her eye. She removed her earphones and gave Zoccola an appraising gaze as he
joined her. "Mr. Zoccola, is it? The business consultant?"

"Inteltech," he said, smiling.

"And what, may I ask, is a business consultant doing
here?"

"The American business community has a vested interest in the security of the region, which security, I
understand, is the reason this conference was called."

She didn't look as though she believed him. "You must move in interesting circles," she said simply.

Zoccola directed his attention to Meureudu, who was smiling toward the audience. "As I imagine you do also, Miss Calenda."

She didn't react to his use of her maiden name.

A bearded Moroccan, clearly a man of some importance, had now taken a position at the lectern and was busy welcoming the representatives of the seventy-one nations that had elected to attend. His remarks were brief and noncontroversial, a prelude to the official welcoming speech that the King was set to deliver.

Again the military band struck up, this time with a martial air to accompany Hassan's imminent appearance.

Escorted by his military staff, all of them bemedaled and beribboned, the King made his grand entrance to the accompaniment of applause.

Adrienne regarded Zoccola with amusement. "Aren't you going to listen to what he has to say? I'm sure the American business community will be anxiously awaiting your report."

"I suppose I ought to." He lifted the earphones to his head.

Now speaking, the King was calling for restraint in the area and was warning foreign powers not to involve the nonaligned nations in their conflicts. "The Maghreb will not be used as a stage on which to mount global war," he declared confidently.

By contrast, when Tunisian Prime Minister Kalek reached the podium, he unleashed an impassioned denouncement of Libya, calling on Qaddafi to pull back his troops while at the same time conceding that his country confronted a grave crisis. "We will soon be taking our case to the United Nations Security Council," he said, "so that we can reveal the details of this villainous conspiracy to destroy our national sovereignty."

Scarcely had he begun the next sentence when a security officer, positioned below the stage and slightly off to the right, fixed his submachine gun on him and fired.

As Kalek's chest turned red and he toppled to the floor of the stage, pandemonium gripped the delegates, and other men, some in uniform, others in plain clothes, opened up on the dignitaries on stage, catching them in a murderous crossfire.

Loyal officers sprang to the King's side, pushed him to the floor, and threw themselves on top of him. Prime Minister Diab tried to find shelter but was cut down by gunfire, and he lay motionless, blood oozing from his ears and mouth.

In spite of the chaos they were causing, it was evident to a shocked John Zoccola that the attackers were targeting only those moderate Arab leaders who stood in opposition to the Libyan advance into Tunisia. Yet the intensity of the assault was such that other Third World leaders present on the stage were struck by random bullets just because they were in the wrong place at the wrong time.

In a moment the shooting stopped and Zoccola's trained mind raced to analyze the situation. He assumed the assailants were Libyan-backed radicals, who weren't especially concerned with whom they killed. After all, these delegates were here in Fez at the behest of King Hassan; only those who supported his position had accepted the invitation and, to the minds of the radicals, they all deserved to die.

It wouldn't have surprised Zoccola if these fanatics didn't hope to foment a revolution that would race like brushfire from one country to another.

But what their ultimate goals were, it was for the moment impossible to determine. In the observation area, shock and bewilderment were visible on the faces of those on all sides of Zoccola. Everyone seemed to be waiting for someone else to react, but there really wasn't any appropriate response to this madness. When the firing began again, those in the press area finally recognized their danger and flung themselves down beneath their desks.

Adrienne continued standing up in an effort to see what had happened to her husband, who was no longer in sight, but Zoccola grabbed her bodily and forced her to the floor. "You'll get yourself killed," he said sharply.

Zoccola didn't take his own advice, and again raised his head to see better. Although the firing had ceased, the hall was still in chaos; desks and chairs had been overturned, and thousands of glass fragments strewed the floor, glinting in the fluorescent lights like jewels. From a distance it was impossible to distinguish the living from the dead, for as a matter of survival the former were imitating the latter.

Some of the assailants had taken up positions at strategic intervals around the hall, effectively sealing it off. While they had suspended their firing, they continued to train their weapons on the hundreds of cowed delegates they held at bay. On the stage several men writhed in pain, shrieking for an end to their lives. After a time two of the gunmen walked up the steps to the stage and methodically delivered coups de grace to any pro-Moroccan leaders they found still alive. They discharged their guns so close to the victims' heads that the shots sounded muffled to those in the press booth.

"We have to do something," Adrienne said desperately. Her voice was practically gone and she spoke in a whisper.

Zoccola agreed that this was a reasonably good idea. But when several of the reporters attempted to leave; two severe-looking guards wearing uniforms of the Moroccan armed forces blocked their passage. Since the assailants had relied on uniforms of the several national security services to infiltrate the conference, there was no telling whose side these guards were on—whether they meant to keep the observers from harm or keep them from escaping.

21

Until the news about the attack on the National Handicrafts Center reached him in the communications room of the Banc Union-Reserve, Drexell had been primarily concerned with keeping abreast of events in the south of Morocco. Outbreaks of fighting between the Moroccan armed forces—the FAR—and Polisario insurgents had been reported in Bou Graa and Semara in the Triangle, in Dakhla on the coast, and near the provisional capital of Hausa. The first reports were sketchy and often contradictory. Frequently, communication was impossible; crucial telephone links were down in Agadir, presumably cut by the guerrillas, and Drexell was obliged to wait for information transmitted back by AWACs and C-130 Hercules observation planes, which were often far from the sources of conflict.

Not only was communication hampered within the region, but Drexell also had difficulty getting through to Washington. In spite of the array of sophisticated technology placed at Drexell's disposal, there were periods during the day when he felt like resorting to carrier pigeon to get in touch with the White House. While he wasn't surprised when the international telephone lines didn't work, he couldn't understand why the satellite relay was, for some obscure electronic or political reason, undependable as well.

To add to his frustration, once he did manage to reach the White House later in the afternoon, Morse Peckum informed him that the President was unavailable and would have to get back to him later.

"We've got a goddamn major crisis going on here —ministers assassinated, Tunisia invaded by Libyan forces, Morocco invaded by Polisario forces, and you're telling me the President isn't available? What the hell's he got to do that's more important?"

"I'll tell you what he's got to do that's more important," Peckum snapped. "He's in the War Room with the Joint Chiefs, working out a response to your crisis. As soon as he's free he'll give you a call."

With that, Peckum terminated the connection.

If he couldn't speak to the President, he at least expected to be able to contact Hahn or Shaw or Hunt—anybody, for Chrissakes, with the commando unit in Libya, but since the initial go-ahead signal had been confirmed, he hadn't been able to raise them again to find out whether the strike on the ORTAG base had achieved its objective or not.

Now, each time one of the signal men monitored Charlie's predesignated frequency, he was rewarded with static and the drone of white noise.

"Keep trying," Drexell said, controlling his frustration.

The paucity of accurate information wasn't confined to the interior of Libya, or the south of Morocco, or the Tunisian border. Even determining what precisely was going on half a dozen blocks away, at the National Handicrafts Center, was near to impossible.

He'd been told by Moroccan authorities that in the first few minutes of the terrorist attack, King Hassan had managed to escape and had now gained sanctuary at his palace, his safety insured by hundreds of loyal, well-armed troops. But this was about the only solid piece of information in Drexell's possession.

Otherwise, all he knew was that the Handicrafts Center was surrounded by Moroccan security forces, who awaited the initial demands of the assailants in order that they could open negotiations.

So for hours now, all he had been able to do was guess at the progress of this dangerous region-wide conspiracy, executed by Libya and fostered by the Kremlin.

Although the assassination attempt against Hassan had failed, there was no telling how many other leaders from pro-Western nations assembled at the conference had been slain. And it might not do any good whatsoever if Hassan had survived should the Polisario attacks in the south succeed in driving the Moroccan army back. With the army in disarray, the revolutionaries could seize the country practically unopposed.

At the same time, Libyan forces might soon overrun Tunisia. Drexell had to hope that on the one hand the Moroccans would be able to counter the Polisario and that on the other the Tunisians, with generous assistance from the U.S. and France, would be able to thwart the Libyan encroachments.

He realized that this was a great deal to hope for, but hope was all that was left to him at the moment.

Ironically, the most reliable information, at least the most coherent presentation of information, was being provided on an hourly basis by the BBC's English and French language broadcasts to North Africa.

"Where the hell are they getting their news from?" Drexell wondered aloud. But none of the other assets he had spoken to, borrowed from the CIA and French intelligence, could give him a satisfactory response.

"Somebody get on the phone to the BBC in London and see how they heard Dakhla was taken by the Moroccans. We've got no confirmation of that."

The BBC man who took the call in London was either unable or unwilling to divulge their source for the story.

A little while later, a further report from the British network stated the following: While the progress of the fighting in the Western Sahara was uncertain, seeming at one point to favor the Polisario and at another the Moroccans, preliminary indications were that the guerrilla offensive was faltering. Unable to make any headway into Morocco, the Polisario was reduced to defending territory previously seized in the Western Sahara. Their tentative gain in the Jbel Quarkziz area was wiped out an hour later by the Moroccans' retaking the garrison of Bir-Anzaran, which they had lost several years previously, and opening up the road to Dakhla to government forces.

There was no question that the war in the Western Sahara would persist for several more days, but one striking note of encouragement emerged in a later BBC broadcast; a representative of the Saharan Democratic Republic—one Mohammed Nazir—was reliably quoted as saying that a UN-imposed truce might be in the best interest of all parties.

"If that's true," Drexell told Cavanaugh, "it means that they've realized they're in a no-win situation. The Moroccans are holding better than they expected they would."

Of course, there was a very good reason that they were holding; apprised of the Polisario battle plans in advance, courtesy of Maxim Kolnikov, the Moroccans had been able to outmaneuver their foe and, in some cases, launch preemptive strikes. In addition, the King, certain that the U.S. Congress would approve a fresh military package for his country, had thrown his most advanced weaponry—and his most elite forces—into the conflict. And the fact that the Americans had previously loaned him C-5 cargo jets to transport his troops to the region and supplied him with reconnaissance and observation aircraft was crucial to the initial success of the Moroccan army.

But success in the south wasn't matched by success to the east. The same BBC news broadcasts that told of Moroccan victories also told of Tunisian reverses. According to the BBC, the Libyan forces had advanced to a position twenty miles inside Tunisian territory, but had suddenly ground to a halt. The reasons for the halt were unclear. At the same time, rioting in the cities and larger towns of Tunisia had spread to the outlying villages. There was no way of knowing who was really in control; Social Democrats, trade union leaders, and Islamic revolutionaries alike were all calling for revolution and claiming that the general uprisings were in support of their particular aims. While Drexell suspected that it was the Islamic elements who had the upper hand, there was no denying that the entire country was united in demanding the ouster of the current regime. Lacking civilian backing, the army was crumbling from within. Those scattered engagements with the Libyans being reported more often involved French contingents than Tunisian forces.

At 7:15 p.m. in a broadcast monitored from Tripoli, a spokesman for the Revolutionary Council of Libya announced that, given the prevailing circumstances, no merger between the nations of Libya and Tunisia would take place "until questions of mutual concern are resolved."

"It's for public consumption," Drexell said to his aide when he read the translation. "The Russians probably leaned on Qaddafi and told him to cool it. Not that it matters. His supporters have gotten just about everything they wanted anyway. A merger can be postponed for a while with no problem to the Libyans."

As if to confirm his words, the gray shortwave radio on the shelf above his head crackled with the voice of the Tunisian Mullah, proclaiming the triumph of the Islamic revolution there.

Drexell had heard enough of the Mullah's shrill demagogic voice over the past week, and he switched to another wavelength.

The passage of five minutes brought a courier into the communications room with word that the Bourguibas, mother and son, had fled Tunisia and were on their way to France where, it was said, they would form a government in exile.

"The hell with the Bourguibas. What's happened to Lisker?"

"Still nothing on him, sir."

After reporting to Drexell about events in Tunis, Lisker was supposed to have been airlifted out by U.S. helicopters along with the last remaining U.S. embassy personnel. This was supposed to have taken place early that morning but thus far there had been no confirmation of it. Having been under orders to link up with Drexell in Fez, Lisker was undoubtedly finding it difficult to reach the ancient capital due to the warlike conditions prevailing throughout Morocco.

With Hahn in the air and Lisker out of touch on the ground and Zoccola held prisoner inside the National Handicrafts Center, Drexell had only his aide, Lieutenant-Colonel Cavanaugh to rely upon. At least temporarily, the entire Task Force was out of commission.

It was almost eight and he also hadn't heard from the White House. Ignorant of what was happening with the Sixth Fleet or the *Nimitz*, Drexell still didn't know if the President had decided to finally go ahead with the military maneuvers and the reconnaissance overflights.

Feeling fatigued by the draining, stultifying tension, Drexell decided not to remain any longer in the communications room of the Banc Union-Reserve, but to go to the National Handicrafts Center even though it was clear his presence wouldn't solve anything there. He instructed Cavanaugh to summon him should anything of importance develop in his absence.

"Mainly, what I want to know is, where the hell's the goddamn *Nimitz*?"

As a member of the Black Ace squadron, J. C. Richards was one of the first pilots to take off from the deck of the *Nimitz* and head south-southeast for Libya. He was piloting one of the hundred warplanes kept in the aircraft carrier's hangar, a Falcon F-16A armed with Sidewinder missiles and capable of attaining speeds up to Mach 2.

This was the first time Richards had been on a combat mission since he'd undertaken the reconnaissance of the Libyan-Tunisian border in mid-July that had ended in the fiery death of pilot Lew Sam Jones.

He'd only been told that morning that he was going back over Libya. It was fine with him. He'd welcome an opportunity to engage the same fuckers who'd sent his friend to his grave in the desert.

Thirty fighters in total were sent aloft from the *Nimitz* at 20:18 hours, just after sunset. Proceeding rapidly over the Gulf of Sidra, they fanned out over Libyan territory at their service altitude of sixty thousand feet, and then bore west, skirting the coastline on their way toward the border with Tunisia.

Richards wasn't surprised when his doppler radar system registered the approach of aircraft coming to intercept them. What did surprise him was that it had taken them so long to make their presence known.

By late afternoon those trapped in the National Handicrafts hall were concerned less with bullets than with boredom. The trapped delegates had gradually picked themselves off the floor to wait in trepidation at their desks, but the assailants made it amply clear, sometimes with cautionary bursts of gunfire into the air, that they were not to move—even to relieve themselves. The fear that gripped some of the delegates was such that they couldn't hold back, and so to the oppressive odor of blood and sweltering flesh was now added the stench of excrement.

There was still no sign of Adam Meureudu, though Adrienne had scanned the hall many times looking for him.

She and Zoccola had more or less made themselves at home in their confined circumstances. He had removed his tie and jacket and unbuttoned his collar, and she had taken off her jacket, although she was still uncomfortable, with perspiration soaking through her white blouse and gluing the fabric to her skin.

"I imagine our hosts have turned off the air conditioning in hopes of stifling us permanently," he said, only half joking.

"They're doing a damn good job of it," Adrienne agreed. "We'll die of dehydration if they don't finish us off with bullets."

She stood up once more to look for her husband.

"I can't imagine where he went," she said.

"I'm sure he's all right. He seems like a real survivor."

She shot a strange look at him, uncertain whether he

meant something pejorative. But all she said was, "I suppose you're right. He's survived worse than this."

Zoccola admitted he wouldn't have minded if her husband had met his end in the firestorm, but he was, of course, too tactful to reveal such a sentiment.

"How much longer do you think this will go on?" she asked.

"I wish I knew. I bet these jokers started out knowing what they wanted to do, and when they got in here and did it, they surprised the hell out of themselves. Now that they're on a roll, they don't know what to demand next."

"Surely they must have had an escape plan."

"Not necessarily. They probably thought they were going to die with their victims. Now that they're not martyrs they're at a loss."

And they certainly seemed to be. From time to time several of the gunmen would drift up to the stage and converse in loud tones among themselves, apparently deliberating as to what step they should take next. They never seemed to reach an agreement.

By early evening, Adrienne was betraying a certain listlessness due to hunger and thirst. Feeling in desperate need of a cigarette, she finally broke her resolution and cadged one from a reporter from Senegal who didn't appear too composed himself. After thanking the man, she said to Zoccola, "You'd think the authorities would send some food in for us."

"They're not even thinking about us. They're only concerned with putting pressure on our captors. We're irrelevant to the equation."

Somehow Hassan had succeeded in escaping from the National Handicrafts Center in the first confused moments of the siege. Now all Morocco was tuned to the national radio, listening to his recorded voice, repeated every fifteen minutes, conveying his assurances that he was still in command of the situation and that he was forming a new government immediately. He proclaimed great victories in the south against the Polisario, pronounced the imposition of martial law, and warned that all dissidents and agitators would be rooted out and dealt with promptly by martial law authorities.

Seemingly because of the King's survival, protests in most of Morocco's major cities began to subside as the day wore on into evening. By nightfall it was reported that the army had managed to return order to the largest population centers.

But the crisis at the National Handicrafts Center went on.

Hundreds of troops ringed the building and ambulances and fire engines were as numerous as armored personnel carriers and half-tracks.

Army snipers had taken up position on neighboring rooftops, training their guns down on the windows and doorways of the center.

Periodically one of the attackers would materialize in a window to observe the situation outside. It was always the same one—a slender man in black, wearing a mask with slits cut out for eyes and lips.

Osman Anzour, a Moroccan general who looked glum even when life was going well for him, had been appointed as chief negotiator. He was terribly patient, capable of letting days pass, if that was what was required, to get his own way.

Hours after the siege began, the negotiator for the radicals finally appeared in the main entrance to the center. He had a Makarov pistol strapped to his hip and constantly rested his hand on it as if for reassurance.

Anzour went to meet him and was told that, to get any hostages released, King Hassan would have to resign in favor of a radical government, the constituents of which he refused to name, since he hadn't discussed them yet with his brothers.

Anzour told him that this was impossible.

Since then, not an hour had passed without some new demand being made, each more bizarre than the last. Anzour replied each time that there could be no concessions until the radicals agreed to release at least some of the hostages.

The radical negotiator eventually said that he would discuss this possibility with his comrades. Four hours went by. It wasn't until after eight in the evening when he appeared again.

"We will release all the women and any wounded if you provide us with five million U.S. dollars and safe passage to Tripoli."

Anzour had been expecting something like this. "If you show us your goodwill and release the women and wounded right now," Anzour said, "then we will give you safe passage to Tripoli."

"What of the money?"

"You should consider yourselves fortunate to be offered sanctuary."

Anzour wished that he could see the man's face behind his mask; the other's expression might give him some idea of how much progress he was making. All he had to go by now was the man's monotonous tone of voice.

"It is possible that we might come to terms," the radical said at last. "I will have to check." He went back inside.

Somewhere just west of Zurawah, the last significant Libyan town before the Tunisian border, J. C. Richards noticed the first wave of Floggers on his right. MiG-

23U's, they were specially equipped with infrared homing devices useful in close combat.

One of the Floggers detached itself from its squadron and banked to the right to head him off. It launched an air-to-air missile, but it was aimed too low and the Falcon was easily able to evade it.

Richards was in his element and was beginning to enjoy the engagement. He dived, swooping down below the Flogger even though he knew the Soviet craft was designed to engage the enemy below its own cruising altitude. "Fuck you, asshole!" he cried out, manipulating the controls that activated the 20mm multibarrel cannon located on the left side of his fuselage.

Raising his eyes, he noted that some of his fellow fighters had gone into action against the Soviet craft. A sidewinder missile launched from one soared into the air, a dazzling sight against the blue backdrop of the darkening sky, and homed in on a Flogger-E. The plane was unable to avoid the missile, which struck it on its cone. The nose sheared off and the Flogger burst into flames and went into a tailspin.

No sooner had this happened when a MiG-23S, a combat jet with a capacity to track and engage targets flying below its own altitude, swept overhead. With its laser ranger and doppler navigator, it was far more of a match for the F-16's than the Flogger-E.

The MiG launched an air-to-air missile—a radar-homing Apex—which went in search of the American jet, found it, and obliterated it.

The air battle was also intensifying in other parts of the sky when the American squadron commander broke radio silence to convey an urgent order. "This is Lima Apple Blue," he said, identifying himself by code name. "We are breaking off now. All units are instructed to disengage and return to base."

J. C. Richards was annoyed. He was just getting

ready for more action and couldn't understand why the show was being called off. He thought they were to continue fighting all the way across the border.

"Break off all combat action immediately," Lima Apple Blue ordered again and gave a course that would put them out over international waters in less than five minutes. Even now Richards could discern the black ribbon of the Mediterranean.

He switched to transmit. "Lima Apple Blue, this is Ranger-One. What gives? Over."

"What gives, Ranger-One, is that those are *Russkies* in those MiG's, not Ayrabs. Over."

"Oh, shit."

"We've got what you might call an international fucking incident on our hands, Ranger-One. Over and out."

Adrienne and Zoccola could barely maintain consciousness. The combination of heat, airlessness, and fear was acting almost like a narcotic on them, and while he still welcomed the opportunity to be with Adrienne, these were not exactly the circumstances he'd envisioned for a tête-a-tête.

In the hall below, the terrorists were exhibiting increased restlessness, repeatedly turning their guns toward the fearful delegates without provocation, simply because they were bored and afraid themselves. Obviously they'd expected nothing like this long wait. They had thought that, if all had gone well, there would have been a general uprising and hours before they would have been paraded out into the streets of Fez, hailed by the masses as heroes and leaders of the new revolutionary government. Instead they were trapped, reduced to trying to salvage their own worthless lives.

While Zoccola had no way of knowing what was happening outside the National Handicrafts Center, he deduced that events were clearly not proceeding the way the terrorists had hoped.

Occasionally one or the other of them would proceed to the lectern and deliver an unintelligible speech about imperialists and corruption, raising the volume of the microphone to such a level that the glass partition above Zoccola's head shuddered with the vibration.

The man who was speaking now, an intense young man with feverish eyes and wearing a camouflage jacket and brandishing a Kalashnikov, was threatening them all with extinction. "You are servants of the Great Satan," he was saying, "and enemies of God and you must pay for this. You have supported the corrupt regimes of Hassan, of Bourguiba, of Sadat and Mubarak, of the Shah . . ."

Adrienne turned to Zoccola and asked him if he thought that the man was serious. Would he, as soon as he concluded his speech, go out into the audience with his comrades and line up all the delegates and reporters and execute them?

"I don't think so," Zoccola replied drowsily. "They're just marking time. They shoot us, their protection is gone."

"I hope you're right." She stared at the speaker, but her attention wasn't really focused on him. "Tell me the truth, John. You're not a businessman, are you?"

"Of course I am," he insisted, rousing himself somewhat.

"You're with some kind of intelligence organization. I can tell. My father was with the OSS, you know. I met a great many of his friends and colleagues. I got so that I can recognize the type."

"Believe what you want." He dug out a business card, which identified him as a representative of Inteltech and gave it to her.

"Is this supposed to convince me? Just think, we may die and you'll never have told me the truth."

"No one's going to die."

"You say that with such assurance. How do you know?"

"Luck," he said, suddenly feeling cocky. "I've always been lucky." He smiled.

"You'd be surprised," he went on, noting her disbelieving look. "Besides, we *can't* die. I still have to buy you that drink I promised."

"Where are we going to have that drink?" she asked, her interest piqued.

"Wherever in the world you'd like. Rio. Singapore. Rome. Katmandu."

"You go where you please? Your company must like you."

"Oh, my company likes me a great deal."

At that moment there was a clamor below, punctuated by shouts and a loud pop that Zoccola guessed to be an explosion.

Then all the lights went out, throwing the entire hall into blackness. Screams welled up from below, followed by successive bursts of gunfire.

Zoccola seized hold of Adrienne's hands and pulled her down just before the observation window shattered with a spray of automatic fire, covering both of them with glass splinters that cut into the exposed parts of their necks, arms, and hands. Zoccola held her protectively, breathing in the smell of her fear.

In the auditorium the terrorists were retreating to one side of the stage, leveling their weapons at the Moroccan forces streaming into the auditorium. In the absence of light no one could be sure exactly where they were firing. But the terrorists still managed to slay several of the men who entered first, catching the rest with a furious salvo that left them scattered.

Soon there were so many bodies of Moroccan troops on the floor that they created an actual barrier to those following after them. Even so, the troops managed to continue firing steadily in the direction of the terrorists.

Three of the latter were struck, one after another, with huge chest and abdomen wounds. With terrible screams, all three fell to the floor. One struggled to get up again, only to receive a broadside to the face, the top half of which instantly caved in. He fell back with his arms extended, his mouth making fishlike sucking noises for a while before becoming still.

The remaining terrorists attempted to escape through the opposite door. But they only ended up confronting yet a second force of Moroccan soldiers, who advanced with M-16's blazing.

Escape cut off, the terrorists clustered in a circle on the stage in a last suicidal show of resistance.

Five more Moroccan troops were killed as they tried to approach the terrorists, who were now slipping grotesquely in the blood that covered much of the floor.

For the most part, the delegates avoided the fury of the battle by remaining down behind their desks. But one delegate from Pakistan was curious and poked his head up over his desk. A bullet creased his skull and turned his hair bloody. Though it wasn't a serious wound, he screamed loud and plaintively, as if he were dying.

Meantime, one of the Moroccan commanders decided not to risk any more of his men and, releasing the pin, rolled a grenade along the floor toward the knot of terrorists.

One spied it, shouted, and groped for it—but too late. It erupted and in doing so, blew apart six men, jettisoning heads, arms, and parts of legs into the air in a cloud that was half smoke and half blood.

When the smoke cleared, it was virtually impossible

to distinguish one body from the other. They lay in a heap, limbs and torsos clustered together. A head with a black beard smeared with blood had been deposited on top of a nearby desk where it remained ignored for hours afterward. In the clump of bodies one terrorist's hand and leg were twitching. One of the Moroccans walked over to the hand, grasped it, then calmly separated it from its owner with his bayonet. He ignored the blood spurting onto his uniform as he accomplished his goal.

Then it was over and the auditorium lights were back on, revealing the extent of the carnage to those who dared raise their heads.

Greater numbers of Moroccan security personnel were coming in now, guns leveled, ready for an opposition that failed to materialize. In moments they were followed in by medical personnel carrying stretchers and wheeling emergency equipment.

Zoccola helped Adrienne up. Their blood was all over them—and her blouse was ripped in several places. "Are you badly hurt?" he asked with acute concern.

She managed a feeble smile. "I don't think so," she said, examining the cuts and plucking out a small shard of glass from her hand. "It's your luck," she told him. "It seems to have rubbed off on me."

22

JULY 31
WASHINGTON, D.C.

The President was in the west wing of the White House conferring with Congressional leaders on the crisis in North Africa when Morse Peckum interrupted him to say that a new emergency had arisen.

Excusing himself, he accompanied Peckum back to the Oval Office. There, Defense Secretary Marty Rhiel, employing a map of North Africa and the Mediterranean, quickly briefed him about the latest incident over Libyan territory.

"There's no question that there were Russian pilots in those MiG's," he concluded. "That's been confirmed."

"Have we heard anything from Moscow yet?"

"Nothing so far. But we're seeing intensified activity from the Black Sea Fleet. Our aerial reconnaissance indicates that a significant number of warships are being detached from the fleet and are now on a course that will put them within shooting distance of the Sixth Fleet at approximately fifteen hundred hours tomorrow."

"Christ," the President replied.

"I think we'll be hearing from our friends in the Kremlin before that happens, though," Peckum offered.

"What's the situation like in Tunisia?" the President demanded.

"Hard to tell how it'll fall into place," said Rhiel, "but there's basically no one there we can depend on. The new government's complexion is more or less pro-Libyan. Whether it's an actual surrogate for Qaddafi or will toe a more independent line remains to be seen. The only silver lining is that the Libyan army is pulling back—they stopped twenty, twenty-five miles inside Tunisian territory several hours ago, and the picture we're getting from people on the ground and satellite recon is that they're now in the process of withdrawing. Maybe the strike on the ORTAG base gave Qaddafi pause, made him hesitant about continuing the advance. Then too the air clash might have convinced him to call the whole show off, especially since, according to the Russian agent, the Soviets wouldn't back him to the hilt. The best I can say is that the situation in Tunisia is highly fluid at this point. The situation in Morocco, on the other hand, looks like it's stabilizing."

"Well, that's something . . ." the President mused.

As concerned as the President was about Tunisia, it was clear that he now had to concentrate his attention entirely on the air battle that had taken the lives of both American and Soviet pilots.

He buzzed his secretary and told her to find Bailey Myers for him. As the most proficient Russian-language interpreter available at State, he was on call twenty-four hours a day so long as any crisis lasted and was never more than half an hour away from the White House.

Twenty minutes later, Bailey was standing in the Oval Office.

Another forty minutes passed before Alexei Kadiyev could be reached in Moscow. The President sensed that the Russian was deliberately stalling him, but there was no reason to make an issue of it. Too much was at stake.

The exchange of formalities was coldly polite.

Kadiyev then proceeded to accuse the United States of playing a dangerous and provocative game. "You are holding mankind hostage," he declared through his interpreter, a man with a voice for mortuaries and late night telephone calls. "By introducing your battleships and your fighter jets into North Africa in an attempt to reestablish imperialist hegemony, you are risking a world conflagration."

Turner ignored the rhetoric.

"Mr. Secretary," the President said, abruptly cutting him off, "it is because of your machinations and your military intervention in the area that we've reached this perilous juncture. We are not about to stand idly by and watch our satellites be shot out of the air nor are we going to allow you or your client states—"

"What client states? We have no client states in North Africa."

"You can't pretend that Qaddafi is not acting in your interests, that without your moral support and willingness to lend military aid, he would undertake an invasion of Tunisia. Nor would the Polisario try overthrowing the legitimate government of Morocco on their own. But that is all moot right now. What matters is that you understand that we cannot permit this kind of interference. I do not want to have a war, nor do I believe that you would place the lives of your own people in jeopardy."

"The threat of nuclear war comes from you alone," Kadiyev said. "It was your pilots, your planes, that violated Libyan airspace."

The President ignored this technicality. "Our intelligence shows clearly that units of the Black Sea Fleet are now heading in the direction of the Sixth Fleet. It would be regrettable if the incident this afternoon over Libya widens into a larger naval conflict in the Mediterranean."

The First Secretary was silent for several moments. The President took this as a signal to continue. "The United States has vested interests in the Mediterranean. To allow anything to undermine these interests would place our allies in Europe in a vulnerable position. You know this as well as I do, Mr. Secretary. We are prepared to take any step necessary to prevent that from happening. The consequences would be entirely your responsibility."

"What is your attitude regarding Tunisia?"

The President realized that the real negotiations were beginning.

"We are not ready to intervene militarily in Tunisia, if that is what you mean. Should Libyan forces fail to completely pull back behind their own borders our position might very well change. And I would expect that pullback to occur within the next twenty-four hours."

What the President was suggesting was a way out of the crisis in which both parties could emerge without losing face. The United States would have certain leeway later in trying to alter the nature of the Tunisian government by either overt or clandestine political means, but it wouldn't send in troops. In conceding Tunisia to Soviet influence, however temporarily, he was indicating that it wasn't worth fighting a global conflict over.

In turn Kadiyev had the option of backing down. It was obviously not an easy thing for him to do. "While my influence with the authorities in Tripoli may be limited, for it is well-known that Mr. Qaddafi behaves as he likes, I will strongly recommend to him that he complete the withdrawal of all his military forces in the time you have indicated."

The Russian's statement wasn't entirely inconceivable. Qaddafi may have actually moved his troops into Tunisia on his own, without Soviet sanction. Perhaps the original Soviet idea had been simply to create the conditions for a revolution in Tunisia, leading to the ascension of a radical regime favorable to Qaddafi; and they had not meant to sponsor a blatant invasion by Libyan forces. Now that the radical regime was in place, the Libyans might not be necessary to keep it propped up. One way or another Qaddafi's troops would have to go.

Kadiyev went even further; he was prepared to offer guarantees. "I will see that no ship of the Black Sea Fleet comes close to ships attached to your Sixth Fleet. If you promise that there will be no future aerial incursions over Libyan airspace, then it is possible that we can bury the incident this afternoon. You are welcome to say whatever you'd like about it, and we shall deny it, of course. Our position is that no Soviet jets or Soviet personnel were involved."

"I think that this compromise might be acceptable."

"Good night, Mr. President."

Kadiyev terminated the connection without waiting for a reply.

The President turned to Peckum and Rhiel. "We'll have to wait and see what happens, but I think we got what we wanted." Despite his cautious words, his mood was plainly elated. "By the way," he asked Peckum with a half-smile, "have we paid Mr. Clean?"

Peckum assured him that the advance on Kolnikov's smuggling operation was now sitting in the Russian spy's Swiss bank account.

"That's good," the President said, nodding his head. "I want him to be happy. I have the feeling we're going to be needing him again quite soon."

23

Early the next morning, William Drexell returned to the Banc Union-Reserve where he found Cavanaugh and Lisker waiting for him.

"When did you get back, Jim?" he asked, his rough voice conveying real pleasure at the other's return.

"An hour ago," he replied. He was clearly exhausted, but given the fact that he'd been in peril of his life as he'd sought to escape Tunis earlier that morning, his weariness was understandable.

"There was nothing we could have done to change the outcome there," Lisker explained. "Before I got to Tunis I didn't know the situation had gone so sour. It was when al-Gazzar asked me for sanctuary that I knew we were lost."

The mention of the Tunisian security chief reminded Drexell of the recent bloodbath at the Handicrafts Center. "He's not going to be needing any sanctuary," he said. "He was one of those assassinated last night."

"He won't be missed," Lisker said.

At that moment the door opened and Zoccola stepped in. He brightened when he saw Lisker. "It's been a while, Jim," he said, and the two men shook hands.

"They tell me you had quite a time today," Lisker said, humor showing on his gaunt features.

Zoccola allowed that this was so. "But I enjoyed the company."

Lisker's expression was puzzled.

"Adrienne Meureudu," Drexell explained, surprising Zoccola. The latter gave his chief a questioning look. He had no idea how Drexell had heard about Adrienne.

"It's always a woman, isn't it, John?" Lisker remarked, shaking his head. "I suppose she has a husband somewhere."

Zoccola shrugged. "She used to, at any rate."

"Still does," Drexell said. "His name isn't on the casualty list."

Before Zoccola could respond, Cavanaugh entered the room. "We have some news," he announced.

"Good or bad?" Drexell asked roughly.

"Well, that's hard to say. We just received word from AFSOUTH." AFSOUTH stood for NATO's Allied Forces of Southern Europe, to which the Sixth Fleet was attached. "There was a dogfight over Libyan territory between U.S. and Soviet-piloted jet fighters."

The four men exchanged tense looks but said nothing.

"Go on," Drexell urged.

"Preliminary reports say that one MiG was lost and one of our own F-16's went down before the fighting broke off."

"Anything from the White House?"

"We're still trying to get through," said Cavanaugh. "But State's already released a statement asserting that the F-16 crashed into the Mediterranean as a result of an accident during a routine naval exercise."

"Shit," Drexell rumbled. "How the hell's that going to hold up under scrutiny?"

He was sure that the President had screwed up badly from listening to the half-baked counsel of his aides.

"Well, I wouldn't hazard a guess on that one, sir, but what's interesting is what Moscow says. Tass put out a press release denying that there are any Russians flying planes for the Libyans. The same story is repeated in today's edition of *Izvestia*. For all the denunciations of the U.S., there's no mention of any air battle taking place between the Russians and Americans over Libya or the Mediterranean."

As Drexel thought over his words, he began to relax. "It's just getting too close," he said quietly. "We both moved back this time. One day it's not going to be so easy to stop it."

The door opened one more time and Jerry Hahn walked into the solemn atmosphere of the communications room.

"I'll be goddamned," Zoccola said. "Look who's here."

"I figured you'd gotten lost in the old city of Turis," Lisker said.

Hahn frowned. After having gotten himself lost on the Farm during the military games, he had acquired a reputation he was finding it impossible to live down.

"I don't need this grief, guys," he said, annoyed but not really angry. He took a chair and extracted a sheaf of papers from his briefcase. He told Drexell, "I've drawn up a full report on Undercross. It has to be edited, but I can get it to you tomorrow."

"It must have been successful, Jerry. The Russians backed off."

Hahn said that it was and looked suddenly pleased with himself.

Drexell smiled. "That's all I need to know right now." He stood up and wished the others in the room a good morning, but before he left he turned to Hahn and said, "You know, Jerry, I think you'll turn out all right."

Hahn nodded, grateful for the recognition. It was as much of a compliment as anyone was ever likely to get from William Drexell, and it was all that Jerry Hahn needed to hear. He had come through.

At the same time he realized that the testing had only just begun. While a major confrontation between the Soviet Union and the United States had been averted, in large measure because of the efforts of Triad, it required no prescience to recognize that a new outbreak of fighting involving the forces of East and West was sure to come again soon. Although there was no telling where the next clash would take place, Hahn had not the slightest doubt that Triad would be there.

And of one thing he was certain: when a new crisis did arise, it might be worse—far worse—than the one he'd just survived.

Here's an exciting preview
of the next book in the
COUNTDOWN WW III
series
coming from Berkley in June

NOVEMBER 18-19, 1986
SOUTHERN ALBANIA

Even as the Soviets were responding to Triad's provocative action in northern Greece, they were continuing their mopping-up operations in Albania, attempting to isolate and eliminate all sources of opposition to their takeover.

Six days after Soviet forces had invaded Albania by air and sea, the object of their conquest still eluded them. According to the original battle plan, code-named Zephyr, four days had been allocated to breaking the back of the Albanian army, overrunning all strategic military and industrial installations, and capturing Tirane and other major cities and ports. An additional ten to fifteen days were to be used to consolidate the Soviet victory and to destroy pockets of resistance that were expected to develop when remnants of the people's militia took to the mountains and forests to continue the war. At the same time, a new government of national unity was to be formed, composed of Albanian leaders who were regarded as compliant but not so closely identified with Moscow that they would be deprived of all political credibility. Also called for in the takeover was an immediate infusion of medical and economic assistance, worth eight hundred million rubles (at the time the official exchange rate was one dollar eighty to a ruble), to restore the country's industrial base as quickly as possible. The aid was also meant to mollify some of the more restive elements of the conquered populace while eliminating evidence of war damage. As far as the Russians were concerned, the sooner people put the conflict out of their minds the better.

But things obviously hadn't worked out as well as the designers of Zephyr had envisioned. The principal flaw in the battle plan was that no one had foreseen how stiff the resistance would be. Though outgunned and outnumbered, the Albanian army and militia, together with police and armed civilians, had managed to slow the Soviet advance and, in a few instances, to almost derail it. The Albanians had the advantage of the rough terrain which alone would have given the Red Army difficulty in securing the countryside. And in many of the cities—in Peshkopi in the east, in Shkoder and Lesh in the north, in Berat, Cerrik, and Vlore in the south—Soviet infantry, armed with hand-held rockets and AKS–74 assault rifles, had encountered fierce house-to-house fighting.

The one noteworthy exception was the capital of Tirane, which had fallen relatively quickly late on the night of November 16 following the capitulation of defending Albanian forces. Surrounded and beset by heavy casualties, more than 3,000 men had laid down their arms and were taken prisoner. Eight hours later the first Russian tanks rolled unopposed into Tirane, reestablishing a Soviet presence in the capital after an absence of over twenty-five years. While most of the city's residents stayed indoors, a scattering of people who'd secretly backed the Soviet Union came out into the streets waving small red flags to welcome the invaders. Scenes of this "welcome," filmed by Soviet cameramen, were relayed back to Moscow television studios, there to be drastically edited and that night shown to millions of television viewers around the world. The edited version would give the impression that the welcoming hundreds actually numbered in the thousands. The ordinary Russian might be forgiven for thinking that the Albanians were exultant to have Soviet troops back in their midst.

In spite of the resentment the citizens of Tirane harbored against the Russians, they did not, for the most part, react with violence. Those who wanted to continue fighting had already joined the army or the militia, and several thousand had already fled the city, fearing that it would be razed by bombing and shelling.

But the actual battle for Tirane had taken place several miles away, and the capital was spared the devastation that had occurred to smaller Albanian cities. Since Tirane was the capital and still contained a small diplomatic presence the Soviets were anxious not to turn it into a rubble-strewn battleground. It would make for very bad public relations, indeed.

But elsewhere, especially in the south, the fighting was continuing and growing increasingly bitter as the Albanians dug in for a last-ditch defense, establishing a perimeter that ran roughly from the fortieth parallel, several kilometers south of Gjirokaster, through Delvine and Sarande on the coast.

Colonel-General Yuri Valerin, deputy defense minister and head of the Kiev military district, had been called in to take command of Operation Zephyr after the failure of General A. Pavlinchuk, commander of the

ground forces of the Southern Group of the Warsaw
Pact, to bring the invasion to a successful conclusion on
schedule.

Initially only the Southern Group, stationed in
Hungary, and elements of the Group of Soviet Forces,
Germany, had participated in the invasion on the
ground. (Detachments of marines, special troops,
rocket troops, and motorized rifle troops had been in-
troduced into the theater of war by naval craft belong-
ing to the Black Sea Fleet.) But the obstinate resistance
by the Albanians had now forced Valerin to request
reinforcements from the Northern Group, based in
Poland, as well as from the Czechoslovakia-based Central Group.

But here again unanticipated difficulties were arising.
Anxious to accommodate its ethnic Albanian minority,
the chief party officials in Yugoslavia were making it
known that they would not accommodate themselves to
another massive airlift of troops over their territory.
They implied to the Russians that they might be forced
to initiate some military action, even to the extent of
downing an Antonov plane or two, though they preferred to remain nonbelligerent. The Soviet ambassador
to Belgrade, a hardliner not generally known for his
sense of humor, told the Yugoslavs that any attempt by
Yugoslavian armed forces to interfere with a second
Soviet airlift of men and supplies would be construed as
an act of war to which the forces of the U.S.S.R. and
Warsaw Pact would respond accordingly.

All this said, then, the Soviets did nothing. The three
divisions Valerin wanted were put on alert, but they
didn't go anywhere. Antonov-22's were made ready and
sat waiting on military airfields in Czechoslovakia and
Hungary, but that was all. Sources close to the Kremlin

told Western reporters that the Politburo was divided on the question of whether further airlifts were worth the risk of antagonizing the Yugoslavians and possibly going to war with them about.

The sixth day of the war found James Lisker heading south, his objective to reach the Greek border before Soviet troops could completely seal it off. While his lean, blond New England good looks made him stand out as a foreigner, the chaos that had enveloped the country was so great that no one cared to question his presence. He was just one of thousands of homeless people streaming south, many of whom carried their few possessions in antiquated cars or in caravans of horse-drawn carts. At various intervals along the roads, checkpoints had been established by Albanian militia of obscure allegiance. Often they wore civilian clothes, and their arms ranged from American to Soviet to Czech to Chinese and German. Lisker suspected that many of these men were little more than bandits exploiting the breakdown in order. Security didn't always seem uppermost in their minds; sometimes they didn't even bother checking the identity cards proffered them. It wasn't the person who interested them, but what the traveler had in his possession. Strip searches were conducted not to uncover weapons—although they inevitably were confiscated—but to find jewelry and money. On occasion, when someone protested, these "militiamen" would threaten to shoot him, which usually provided enough inducement to silence even the most unruly refugee.

Needless to say, Lisker repaired to the woods whenever he saw any sign of these brigand roadblocks.

The demarcation line separating the forward positions of the Red Army and the Albanian resistance was always a rather ambiguous thing. A part of the road might be in the hands of the Albanians while five miles down the road a Russian brigade might turn up, with its commanding officer intently studying a map, not yet aware that he was behind enemy lines.

More to demoralize the fleeing population than to accomplish any military goals, the Soviets would daily dispatch attack planes to strafe the roads and the people who were using them. The Russians most often employed MiG-27's—Flogger-G swing-wing craft—for this purpose. Gun and rocket packs were installed in stations under the wings and the pilots used both with abandon.

The people on their long march south soon developed a keen sensitivity to the sound of approaching Floggers, even over the din of the trucks and buses. Usually by the time they appeared, everyone had already leaped to the side of the road for shelter. Those who didn't were often struck by the Floggers' tracer bullets. At night the effect of an attack was particularly startling, every fifth bullet tracing a line of eerie blue light down into the packs of fleeing people. From time to time, cluster bombs were dropped, not so much to kill as to destroy a truck or military vehicle. Most of the few mobile radars of the retreating Albanian force were eventually demolished in this manner. By the time Lisker approached the fishing village of Butrint, which lay at the western edge of the Albanians' last-ditch defense perimeter, all he could think of was finding a warm place where he could sleep for longer than an hour. Even the food his stomach craved didn't appeal to him nearly as much as the idea of a warm bed and undisturbed sleep.

Although there was no one to speak his language, Lisker could see that the small fishing port was being transformed into a final redoubt by Albanian troops.

This close to the Greek border there was practically nowhere to run to. Everywhere Lisker looked in and around the village, he saw Albanian soldiers and militiamen, many wrapped in bandages and with their uniforms in tatters, taking up positions and fortifying them with sandbags. Just to the north of Butrint, a collection of Roman ruins was being converted into fortifications and older tanks of Russian manufacture—mainly sandyellow T34/85's—were being deployed with their hulls sunk into the earth to create a defensive line.

Refugees were camped out in the exposed rice paddies around Butrint, which had been fashioned and formed on the basis of the Chinese model. There was no place in the port itself for all the people. Butrint, which had a surprisingly Greek look, with its whitewashed houses and quaint passageways, had had virtually all of its buildings appropriated by the army. If the Russians intended to take Butrint they would be able to do it only by engaging in house-to-house fighting.

But that night—the night of the eighteenth—the Soviets showed that they preferred to bomb and shell Butrint before sending in infantry. Su-19's—codenamed Fencers by NATO—flew in formation over Butrint and at 10:20 began to deliver a punishing bombing. Fortunately, the refugees who were scattered about the rice paddies escaped the brunt of the bombardment. They watched the spectacle of the port's destruction as if it were a theatrical event, a sound-and-light show that sent brilliantly colored flames surging up from the ruins of Butrint, turning the sky a lurid pink.

Antiaircraft defense was ineffectual, creating a great deal of noise without striking any of the bombers.

As soon as the Su-19's had gone, Antonov transport jets and MiG-14 Haze transport helicopters swept overhead, bypassing Butrint in the direction of the rice paddies. As the doors of the Antonovs opened, they released wave upon wave of paratroopers, who dropped down into the camps of unsuspecting refugees. In the dark the paratroopers had no notion who they were confronting and began to open fire as they landed. In the ensuing confusion people screamed in panic and ran in all directions.

A few armed men among the refugees were able to attack the invaders, taking them as they tried to disengage from their parachutes, slashing their throats with assault knives when no guns were available. But such instances were rare; in most cases, the Albanians fled, slipping in the mud where the ground hadn't frozen yet.

Little by little the Russian forces drew together to concentrate on their primary task: the taking of Butrint itself. In the pandemonium, Lisker was able to escape the quagmire that the rice paddies had become, repeatedly stumbling over the bodies of men and women who had been cut down only minutes before. Bullets whistled overhead and to the side of him. He hurt in many places, but he couldn't stop to check himself. At least he doubted he'd been struck by a bullet—none of the pains he felt was that intense—but it was possible that he had been hit by a piece of shrapnel. Earlier he'd felt something slice into his leg, but he could still move it, and at this point, that was all that counted.

Worse than the bullets was the whine of incoming rockets, reaching their crescendo with explosions that caused the earth to shudder. As he raced, hunkered down, Lisker felt like he was in Nam again—the shrieks of pain, the rockets, the shelling, but most of all the darkness and the chaos.

As he ran he kept his gun in hand although he doubted that it would do him much good. It might give him confidence, but against tanks and rockets he was clearly at a disadvantage.

He suddenly found himself close to the Albanian tank position. He had always been of a mind that tanks should be used offensively. The evidence before him seemed to bear him out. Of the eight tanks—the most modern was a T-62—six had been thoroughly demolished, and even the two more or less intact tanks were obviously out of commission.

In the exchange, two Russian T-72 tanks had been hit and abandoned approximately fifty yards away from the former Albanian position.

The Russian tanks must have been moved up the previous night and concealed until the airborne attack was launched, Lisker guessed. And from the way it looked the attack was still continuing as parachute flares popped, one after another, revealing a sky full of descending paratroopers. The Soviets were obviously stopping at nothing to put an end to all resistance in the south, and there was no reason to think they wouldn't succeed.

For Lisker the only thing that still mattered was getting over the border. He reckoned that he was, at most, a single day's walk from it. But in these circumstances there was no telling what a single day could bring or whether he would last long enough to see the next evening. As he finally arrived at the edge of the rice fields, strobe lights flashed across the battlefield, and Butrint itself produced a steady orange glow as its buildings and streets were engulfed in flames. And still the pounding by artillery persisted, causing structures in the port to collapse on the men who'd fortified themselves inside.

Little by little the paratroops from the rice paddies and the infantry units coming in from the road began to move into port, assault rifles blazing. Clashes were still going on in the middle of the ancient Roman ruins, but already the decimated Albanian force was pulling back, attempting to fade into the woods exactly as Lisker was doing.

By dawn Lisker was zigzagging through a dense forest that reminded him of the one he'd entered several nights previously with Hahn. Here, though, it wasn't quite so mountainous. He was exhausted, the pain in his leg much worse, and there was a numbing sensation in his calf that he tried to ignore. Blood was collecting in his right shoe, and when he finally inspected the shrapnel wound, he discovered that a great deal of skin on his calf had been shredded and the muscle exposed. His emergency kit had been stolen while he slept, so he improvised a tourniquet from a spare shirt he carried in his ration bag. Occasionally in his painful trek toward the border with Greece, he came across others in flight. Words were seldom exchanged, just small gestures—a quick nod of the head, a darting of the eyes—to acknowledge their common plight.

The sounds of war followed him through the woods and into the occasional open valley. He could frequently hear distant artillery fire, but he also recognized the sound of 73mm guns from BMP infantry combat vehicles. It sometimes seemed that the war was still north of him and at others that the worst fighting was in the west or even in the south, where he was headed.

Late the next afternoon, he knew that he had at last reached the border when he saw strands of barbed wire threaded through the landscape.

In several places the barbed wire had been broken through or simply ripped down, probably by the border guards themselves in pursuit of refugees. While mines were undoubtedly planted throughout the no-man's-land, the border guards had clearly tramped down a path that avoided them. A rolling field obstructed by occasional clumps of brambles, the area appeared free of Russians, and any other human presence besides James Lisker.

Unfortunately, he couldn't see all the way into the Greek side of the frontier. After running through the rolling field, the no-man's-land vanished into a thicket of brush and waist-high grass. A guard tower—apparently deserted now—stood to the far left of where Lisker was standing, but whether this guard tower belonged to the Greeks or the Albanians he couldn't determine.

Midway across the no-man's-land, he detected the sound of men's voices. He stopped for an instant and turned to see at least a dozen soldiers deployed about 200 yards behind him along the rise he'd just come down. The red stars on their uniforms and helmets identified them as Russians. As they looked down into the no-man's-land through binoculars, one of them spotted Lisker and called sharply to him to halt.

He didn't halt. He figured his chances were slightly better if he ran than if he surrendered. By this point he had the brush and the high grass to partially conceal him. As bullets whipped about him, the wound in his right leg stung savagely, but still he plunged on.

About the Author

W.X. Davies is the pseudonym of a well-known writer. He took on this new series both to entertain and to argue for a more sophisticated espionage capability for the U.S.

The Strategic Operations Group is an informal advisory council whose military, intelligence and security experience provides much of the background for the series.